Larkin at Sixty

Larkin at Sixty

Edited by
ANTHONY THWAITE

faber and faber

First published in 1982
by Faber and Faber Limited
3 Queen Square London WC1N 3AU
Printed in Great Britain by
Latimer Trend & Company Ltd Plymouth

British Library Cataloguing in Publication Data

Larkin at sixty.
1. Larkin, Philip—Criticism and interpretation
I. Thwaite, Anthony
821'.914   PR6023.A66Z

ISBN 0-571-11878-x

Contents

7

CONTENTS

Illustrations

ILLUSTRATIONS

Introduction

In Barry Bloomfield's magisterial *Philip Larkin: A Bibliography 1933–1976*, the initial date gave me a bit of a surprise when I first noticed it. *1933*? The poet whose sixtieth birthday is celebrated in the present book was, as a little sum-doing makes plain, born in 1922. Was Larkin, then, of that precocious company that includes Abraham Cowley, Alexander Pope ('I lisp'd in numbers, for the numbers came') and Thomas Chatterton?

Recourse to Mr Bloomfield's bibliography shows a single entry for 1933, under 'Contributions to Periodicals': 'Getting up in the morning. *The Coventrian*, 143 (December 1933, 965)'. I have forborne to search the archives of King Henry VIII School (a place memorialized here by Noel Hughes) for this effort by the eleven-year-old P. A. Larkin; though its title suggests, probably wrongly, a proleptic version of that chilling poem of some forty-five years later, 'Aubade'. One has to balance Larkin's own contention that he was a tardy developer against the scatter of listed contributions to *The Coventrian* from 1933 to 1940, the year he left the school and went up to Oxford; and balance it, too, against the strikingly efficient Audenesque of his sonnet 'Ultimatum', published in the *Listener* in November 1940 during his first term at St John's.

The man for whose birthday this book has been assembled has been characterized (by a critic who judged his *Oxford Book of Twentieth Century English Verse* to be 'a calamity') as 'the best-loved poet of his generation'. Many would call him the finest living poet writing in English. But epithets and superlatives like these look inept, overblown, in the light of that wry, mocking and self-mocking regard to which several of the book's contributors draw attention. Philip Larkin is not puffed up with that monstrous gigantism which tends to infect even good poets who have won whatever 'fame' means in the world of contemporary poetry.

On the other hand there is no mock modesty about him either. Those interviews with him which have become public through publication (more of these than seems probable, given such an essentially private man) bear this out. And the man whose attitudes, judgements and self-judgements have been recorded over the years by such interlocutors as Ian Hamilton, Dan Jacobson, John Haffenden and Miriam Gross is all of a piece with the man whose conversation and letters are quoted here by old friends and newer ones too.

These interviews, good though they have been, have no place in this book; nor have any other of the already published pieces on Larkin and his work. What I aimed to do was to invite a number of people to write something new, whether memoir, tribute, some piece of comment on aspects of Larkin's poems, his other writings, his taste, his activities as librarian (and remarkable assiduousness as committeeman, in and out of libraries); and perhaps a poem or two. The result is of course diffuse and patchy, not definitive: this is not *The Life and Letters of Larkin*, a book already part-way to completion by Dr Jake Balokowsky, and waiting only for its subject's demise. Alan Bennett has something to say of the inappropriateness of a birthday book for Larkin, and in the process challenges several of the present book's assumptions. At the same time, Mr Bennett underlines the affection in which Larkin's readers hold him, and the remarkable sense of privilege which they feel at knowing his work. I can think of very few contemporary British (or American) poets whose poems are so substantially known by heart and quoted.

Not everyone who should be here is here. I originally had lined up an American, a Russian, a Pakistani and a woman ('minority enthusiasts', one can hear someone saying); but illness, silence, disappearance and diffidence eliminated them, I am sorry to say. The oldest contributor is seventy-six, the youngest not yet thirty,

and if the majority are 'at that vague age that claims /The end of
choice, the last of hope', well, it somehow seems appropriate;
though my own experience, visiting schools and colleges in
Britain and abroad, has shown me that Larkin's enthusiastic and
devoted audience extends among the young as well as the middle-
aged and old.

The poems can also survive translation, against all the odds. In
Peking I heard a young Chinese lecturer recite his own translation of 'The Whitsun Weddings' in Mandarin, and even an
untutored ear could follow its fidelity of shape and feeling. The
Germans, who gave him their Shakespeare Prize in 1976, recognize and respond to Larkin's *stillen Grundtrauer*, and also quote
with approval Frost's dictum: 'You can't be universal without
being provincial'. In Yugoslavia I have met followers of *'Ulazak
u crkvu'* ('Church going' in Serbo-Croat). Though I may have been
the first to introduce Larkin's poems to Japan in 1955, closely
followed by the publication there of D. J. Enright's pioneering
anthology *Poets of the 1950s*, a return visit in 1980 showed me that
the word has spread. As for the Italians and *'Le nozze di Pentecoste'*
—of course one has to admit that almost anything sounds
marvellous in Italian.

The anecdotes (and the squibs and limericks here published for
the first time, to which friends could add many more, languishing
until the Appendix to *The Complete Works*) represent some sides
—important sides—of Larkin. Clive James, Christopher Ricks,
Seamus Heaney and others in their different ways show other
aspects, distinct but related. Re-reading them all before writing
this introduction, I tried to stand back and see the multifoliate
personality as if I didn't know it at all, or only through the poems.
Some characteristics are variously and even repetitively touched
on and touched in; others seem to me to be absent, or almost so.
The curmudgeonly loather of literature Kingsley Amis knew at
Oxford is still there; but the man whose social exasperation is
triggered off by 'some bitch /Who's read nothing but *Which*' feels
such exasperation because he has read, and goes on reading, a
great deal else, some of it with enthusiasm. The poems of Hardy

and Betjeman, the novels of Anthony Powell and Barbara Pym, are tastes Larkin has allowed to have a public airing, and the danger has been a view of him as someone who has read little but a dozen canonical books. But in fact he has an extraordinarily well-stocked memory, can quote curiously and accurately, and—for all his shunning of the platform and the poetry circuit—is a superb reader of not only his own but others' work. I remember an evening recently at his house in Hull (a comfortable and well-appointed place, where he grumbles about mowing the lawn and the vagaries of his car like any householder) when he and Monica Jones and I tape-recorded, at his instigation, some favourite poems, fortified with a few bottles of wine from the local off-licence.

Nor is he in my experience the undomesticated Bleaney, the child-detesting misogynist, the unsociable Scrooge his *personae* sometimes persuade one into accepting. It's always struck me what a courteous affability he shows to the old, the young, the uncertain, the vulnerable, with a sense of appropriateness which is never put on for the occasion but which is natural to him—as natural as his care for his mother during her long years of widowhood and illness. There is, at a more trivial level, the grave awe with which he confronted a small daughter of mine 'entertaining' him with card tricks, or the solicitude which he brings to establishing that what one normally has for breakfast is a boiled egg and honey, and seeing that they are there on the table. It is possible to maintain (as George Hartley does in his contribution) that Larkin is 'outside all the main emotional entanglements of most people's lives—love, marriage, children'; but it depends what one means by 'entanglements'. The fact that he has never married and has no children doesn't entail ignorance of, or contempt for, the institution or its usual result. As for love, 'that much-mentioned brilliance', even to feel outside it one must know what it is; and he does.

I seem to be working round to a statement that Larkin is really much nicer, much more normal, much more like *us*, than both his admirers and his detractors have established—which would be cosy all round, as well as apparently giving the lie to some of the poems. That is not my intention, though the friendly gesture of a commemorative volume such as this one is of its nature different from that of distant detached biographers. They are not my concern, though no doubt eventually they will find material for contemplation in these pages. The work remains, unassailable except by those who look for something in poetry other than the virtues of startling truth, memorability, skill and poignancy embodied in Philip Larkin's poems. Those who celebrate him here cover a wider spectrum of taste than even I had supposed when I set out to edit this book, in spite of the defections and disappointments I mentioned earlier. He may question the veracity or accuracy of everything included; but all of it comes with warmth—and, indeed, love.

ANTHONY THWAITE

The Young Mr Larkin

NOEL HUGHES

In the preface to the reissue of *Jill*, Philip recalls our spending 'two disrespectful years' in the sixth form. Writing in the school magazine of that same period, a recently retired master remembers him as 'distinguished ... by his exceptional courtesy'. There is no contradiction. Philip was summoning up a mood; Mr Liddiard, a pattern of behaviour. Philip's temptation towards the dangerous life was always held in check by a preference for living it vicariously.

It was in form IIA that I first met Philip. That and IIB (the division was alphabetical) constituted the first year of the senior school of King Henry VIII, Coventry. He would sit over to my left: short-cut hair falling forward toward gold-rimmed glasses, his large head slumped forward more, I suspect, to avoid catching a master's eye than the better to read a book. We would each have considered ourselves as naturally shy. I was finding the transition from an elementary school disconcerting. Philip, arriving from the cosiness of the prep school, was disturbed by what he would later call 'the traumatic influx of scholarship boys'. In common we had, it seemed, nothing more than a profound distaste for all forms of physical activity. That we became friends so soon was due to Colin Gunner, Philip's close ally in the prep school.

Colin was an ebullient chap of classical scrum-half stockiness. His unfailing optimism was sufficient to compensate for our morose anxieties. But he was most remarkable for his unbounded imagination. Though without Kingsley Amis's talent for imitating sickly combustion engines, he played at school the role Kingsley would play at St John's: he could rescue our spirits from the blackest pit.

Each day, after school, we would amble to the foot of Warwick Road, where Philip would walk the few yards to his home, Colin would set off on his bicycle, and I boarded the tram to Foleshill. As we strolled we devised defamatory characters for our masters, situations in which they could be made to appear imbecile, conversations which—if they were as doltish as our re-creations of them—they might conceivably hold together. Occasionally in class a master would approximate to a pre-envisaged role. Then three, seemingly meaningless, and sometimes uncontrollable, shouts of laughter would follow. As we grew older, and the crises of the mid-thirties came upon us, the Warwick Road ambles became more political, especially if we were joined by Frank Smith, a High Anglican for whom, rather improbably, Philip wrote blank verse choruses for a passion play for Holy Week 1939. But whatever the news, we stuck to the slapstick.

It was the Warwick Road ambles that underpinned my friend-ship with Philip, because we were soon parted. Most boys went from IIA (or B) to IIIA (or B). Some went there indirectly through lower III. It was a system that allowed you to fall a year behind, but never to catch up. I went to IIIA, Philip to lower III. We were not to be in the same class again together till the sixth form, where the differences between the years were not pronounced and much work was done in common.

There is a widespread belief, resting partly on legitimate interpretation of his verse, partly on specific indications from Philip, that his schooldays were pretty wretched. In an *Observer* interview with Miriam Gross, Philip asserted he was 'an un-successful schoolboy' and that children were generally 'selfish, noisy, cruel vulgar little brutes'. In a preface that he wrote for Colin's privately published war memoirs, he was more precise: 'I was not happy at school. Admittedly it was an affair of being more frightened than hurt, but it was being hurt sometimes, and being frightened was not very pleasant ... my form position was always well down in the twenties.'

18

Was he really so miserable at school? And if unhappiness did characterize those years, would that be a distinguishing characteristic? The sardonic wit that makes him such a delightful companion has always co-existed with a sense of doom. For Philip to be fully at ease with the world, confident that all the planets are in their proper places, he needs the comforting assurance that his health, finances and career, the national economy and civilization, are all directed undeviatingly towards disaster.

But unsuccessful? There were normally two form prizes, awarded on examination results and therefore favouring the all-rounder that Philip was not. After the minor débâcle of lower III, it was quite a coup for him to take second prize in IIIA. Thereafter, he always took some sort of prize; for three years for his contributions to the school magazine, and in his final year a special prize for general knowledge. This was not given on competition and, if it had been, few would have backed Philip to win it. It represented the determination of the headmaster to reward an exceptional talent that the examination system would surely fail to do.

In general, he was well-liked and quite without enemies: popular with the boys because he mocked the staff, and with the staff because he was invariably polite towards them. It was not a school in which bullying was much evident. Physically, his frame was large and filled out early. When he was finally cajoled into playing for the second xv the games master reported that 'his height and weight ought to make him very useful in both the lineout and the scrum'. In repartee, Philip could always give out better than he got.

It was a tolerant school, as day schools tend to be. On Wednesday afternoons, at least until representative games began to take over, we would go to the cinema. I must have seen *Scarface* with Philip half a dozen times. After war had been declared, and gatherings were considered needless hazards, school attendance became rather fitful. Much work was done at home or in the public library, and essays were often presented in a master's home.

There was an enforced obligation to wear a school cap, and a commonly disregarded one to wear a house tie; there were no other rules of dress. This must have comforted Philip enormously. He would have hated those schools where uniform was compulsory and where the carrying of an umbrella or the sporting of unbuttoned flies could signify rank and seniority. He always dressed well, but soberly; not without elegance, or even panache, but only in such degree as would not compromise maturity. Invariably, and most obviously, he dressed above his years. He was quick into long trousers; nobody that I ever knew took earlier to the trilby. He preferred a watch in his breast pocket to a wristwatch. I recall, later at St John's, a hot and gloriously sunny Saturday morning. Philip was then probing the foothills of the literary establishment, had become college agent for the *Cherwell*, and was outward bound on *Cherwell* affairs. Whether to mark the errand or the splendour of the day, Philip decided to wear beneath his jacket the top from his pyjama suit of broad matching pastel stripes. Somehow he looked more like an old man reaching back for his youth than a young blade breaking out.

But school is only one of the factors in the school years. Time to consider Philip's father, whom he described with rather opaque accuracy to Miriam Gross as 'a local government official'. I do not remember, at school, that Philip ever spoke *about* him. Occasionally, he would contribute to a Warwick Road amble a paternal opinion in a way that implied that it ought to be taken as conclusive. From these occasions I gained no clear impression of the man, but a strong conviction of the awe in which Philip held him. Yet this obscure figure was, in other ways, quite well known to us.

Sydney Larkin, OBE, FRSS, FSAA, FIMTA, City Treasurer of Coventry for more than twenty years was, *ex officio*, a local notable getting his due space in the local press. He was much more than that. Among his fellows (he served his term as president of his professional institute) he was held in the highest esteem as a brilliant innovator, and there were those who went to Coventry to work under him. To these, he was an administrative paragon: always formidably prepared for committee, precise and lucid on paper, a superb delegator, a man who never admitted to being busy. Others recall a different side. To those who fell short of his expectations or were unable to stand up under pressure from him, he could be mercilessly dismissive.

Three other characteristics are significant. He had a great love of English literature, and especially of D. H. Lawrence, and he enjoyed poring over dictionaries, Fowler and Ivor Brown. (He once said of Kingsley Amis that his lack of grasp of *will/shall* and *would/should* precluded his having a future as a writer.) Secondly he was noted for staffing his office with pretty girls (some my contemporaries). Lastly, the cast of his mind was authoritarian. Punctilious though he was in observing the conventions and obligations of English public service he discovered, on his visits to Germany, qualities of decisiveness and vigour in German public administration that compelled his admiration.

Being raised by so forceful a personality (and Sydney's pride in Philip could hardly be exaggerated) was at least as formative and lasting an experience as school. If Philip still thinks of school as a wretched time, I am sure he would have to concede that such comic relief as there was (and he has always needed the occasional shot of it) came from Colin and his school-mates. In contrast, and in spite of the unfailing graciousness of Mrs Larkin's welcome, the atmosphere of Philip's home, with its intimidating tidiness, its highly waxed furniture and the practice of hushed conversation, impressed me as solemn.

There is in Philip much that is reminiscent of his father. I am sure that Sydney would have directed his early reading, and he left Philip with an abiding regard for Lawrence. He must have contributed something to that superb mastery of language that has characterized all Philip's verse. In common, too, there was fastidiousness in dress and a preference for bow ties (which Philip taught me how to tie). There was the urbanity verging on courtliness that Mr Liddiard so early observed. Detached from his father's quirky involvement in politics, Philip has remained instinctively rooted on the right. There is some inheritance in religious matters, though here Sydney's position was perhaps less equivocal. For Sydney combined a total disbelief in Christianity with an admiration for the seemliness of Anglican ceremony on formal occasions, and with such seemliness he was buried.

Religion is one of those matters where Philip and I have been most obviously at variance. Philip has always kept his cards tight to his chest, suspecting, probably without looking, that any God that might exist would have dealt him a Yarborough. I, on varying grounds and with fluctuating ardour, have given a continuing allegiance to Rome. So much was obvious at school because we Catholics and Jews absented ourselves from morning service and scripture. It was during a sixth form history lesson that Philip passed a book under the table, pointed to a paragraph and hissed 'get out of that'. I believe the book to have been an early Joad and the paragraph set out the clear illogicality of any belief in God. I remember being annoyed with myself at the time for not being able to dispose of it.

And then there was the celebration of the fourth centenaries of St John's and Trinity. Champagne flowed freely, and it was clear when Joanna and I arrived that Philip had made an early start. He cantered towards us across the lawn bellowing 'Hello, Noel, have you still got that absurd religion of yours?' As Philip Marlowe would have said, 'There was nothing in that for me.' Eventually we broke up for bibulous supper parties before reassembling for fireworks. Out of the dusk, Philip suddenly appeared. The time had come, so it seemed to me, for us to lie down like Joxer and Boyle and contemplate the surplus of stars. Instead, Philip embarked on an amorous embrace. With an aplomb remarkable in the circumstances, Joanna pulled a flower from a bush to serve as reward and substitute. She did not know that a row of stitching across a lapel is not a certain indication of a buttonhole. As she wrestled to force the stem through solid cloth, Philip could get no closer to explaining the difficulty than muttering 'it's only a Burton's suit'. I thought this a dilemma better to be observed than solved. At least that is the thought I think I would have thought if ratiocination had been easy. I kept the faith with Mr Burton.

Oxford and After

KINGSLEY AMIS

Soon after arriving at St John's College, Oxford in April 1941 I met somebody who, a trifle comically I thought at the time, was called Philip Larkin. I was most impressed with his self-confidence when he told me not very long afterwards that he had once come across in some writers' manual a list of names not to be given to serious characters, and found 'Larkin' on it. At our first meeting, which I remember as much less dramatically satisfying than the account he gives in his introduction to the 1964 edition of *Jill*, his clothes too seemed to me not very serious: tweed jacket, wine-coloured trousers, check shirt, bow tie. In my suburban way I considered them flashy, but I would have had to admit that they were neat, the shoes clean, the tie carefully chosen and knotted. He has always dressed well and smartly, also appropriately, whether in undergraduate informals or the senior librarian's 'good' suits.

He had a biggish nose, a fresh complexion and a head of rather nice light-brown hair that was already, though he was only eighteen then, showing signs of recession. It was again not much later that he said his grandfather had been bald as a coot at twenty-eight. ('He used to wear a cap in the house. He looked ridiculous.') As soon as he opened his mouth he revealed himself as afflicted with a painful stammer (now long since cured) that sometimes hindered communication. Nothing else did. After the initial awkwardness characteristic of the amiable, his manner proved to be friendly, informal, even rather noisy, larded with imitations of public-school men, Yorkshire scholars, assorted rough persons and others.

The art-form I associate with Philip at Oxford was not any sort of literature but jazz. Hitherto I had treated it as one more indisputably good thing along with films, science fiction, the wireless and all that. Philip was passionate about it, as were numbers of his and our friends and as I soon became. I cannot improve on his descriptions (in the introductions to *Jill* and to *All What Jazz*) of the part it played in our lives; I will just add that our heroes were the white Chicagoans, Count Basie's band, Bix Beiderbecke, Sidney Bechet, Henry Allen, Muggsy Spanier, Fats Waller, early Armstrong and early Ellington—amazing that there were early bits of them by 1941—and our heroines Bessie Smith, Billie Holiday, Rosetta Howard ('I'm the queen of everything') and Cleo Brown. One or two of them must be still alive.

About this time the OU Rhythm Club organized a series of concerts, but the material was not much to our liking: George Shearing, Cyril Blake's band from Jig's Club in Soho, the seven-year-old Victor Feldman. Much more congenial, to me, were the sessions at the Victoria Arms in Walton Street, now converted to the uses of the Oxford University Press. Here, in a small dingy room usually empty or nearly so, there was a battered but well-tuned piano which Philip could be persuaded to play. He did so with some proficiency in an unemphatic style that at this distance —I have not heard him perform for a long time—sounds to my mind's ear as much like Jimmy Yancey's as anyone's. The result was graceful, clear, melodic and often faintly sad, the Larkin of 'Coming', if you will, rather than of 'Whatever Happened?' ('How did you learn?'—'Years of trying.') He stuck as a rule to the twelve-bar blues form, which was fine with the rest of us—it was our favourite too. If there were no outsiders present I would sometimes sing, or rather bawl, a series of lyrics culled from records; 'Locksley Hall Blues' (Tennyson—Larkin) was an exception.

Nevertheless literature, in the form of the syllabus of the English School, forced itself upon us both: lectures to attend, essays to write and above all books to read, texts, poems. All Old English and most Middle English works produced hatred and weariness in everyone who studied them. The former carried the redoubled impediment of having Tolkien, incoherent and often inaudible, lecturing on it. Nobody had a good word to say for *Beowulf, The Wanderer, The Dream of the Rood, The Battle of Malden.* Philip had less than none. If ever a man spoke for his generation it was when, mentioning some piece of what he called in a letter to me 'ape's bumfodder', he said, 'I can just about stand learning the filthy lingo it's written in. What gets me down is being expected to *admire* the bloody stuff.' So far, as I say, so standard, but he would have commanded less general support for his equally hard line on Middle English literature, in which others could find a few admirable or at least tolerable bits, mostly by Chaucer. When it came to works in Modern (post-1500) English, he was on his own.

I have no recollection of ever hearing Philip admit to having enjoyed, or again to being ready to tolerate, any author or book he studied, with the possible exception of Shakespeare. He was at best silent even on those who, from the evidence of his own work, might have been expected to appeal to him: Collins, Crabbe, Clare. (The compulsory part of the syllabus stopped before it reached Christina Rossetti, let alone Hardy). During the summer vacation of that year I worked my way through *The Faerie Queene.* Like most of us, I think, I resented having to read it at the required pace, but without being likely to repeat the experience I was quite glad to have been forced into it. Not so Philip. I had used the college library copy (principle as well as finance decreed that you never bought a book merely because you were going to be examined on it). At the foot of the last page of the text he had written in pencil in his unmistakable, beautiful, spacious hand:

First I thought Troilus and Criseyde was the most *boring* poem in English. Then I thought Beowulf was. Then I thought Paradise Lost was. Now I *know* that The Faerie Queene is the *dullest thing out. Blast* it.

(I queried the uncharacteristically non-alcoholic language with him; he retorted that he had not dared to aggravate his offence by writing down the words he was thinking.)

I must not give the impression that such judgements were offered in talk and then to any extent discussed. Whatever one made of it in private, most people at Oxford, not just Philip, treated literature as a pure commodity, something to be manipulated into getting you a degree. Reading it and going to lectures on it was how you prepared for the only significant event, the coming battle of wits with the examiners.

We paid special attention to the Romantics. Each was brought up and dismissed in two lines in 'Revaluation', another blues; they all signed on as Bill Wordsworth and his Hot Six—Wordsworth (tmb) with 'Lord' Byron (tpt), Percy Shelley (sop), Johnny Keats (alto and clt), Sam 'Tea' Coleridge (pno), Jimmy Hogg (bs), Bob Southey (ds). (There was a Café Royal Quintet too, I remember, with 'Baron' Corvo on drums.) Shelley was singled out for a form of travesty in which nothing was altered but much added: 'Music,' began one of Philip's, 'when soft *silly* voices, that have been talking *piss*, die, Vibrates, like a . . .'

I need not go on. If this sort of thing seems the product of quite routine irreverence and high spirits, so be it. To outward view, Philip was an almost aggressively normal undergraduate of the non-highbrow sort, hard-swearing, hard-belching, etc., treating the college dons as fodder for obscene clerihews and the porter as a comic ogre, imitating Tolkien, getting me to imitate Lord David Cecil, going to the English Club but treating its sessions as incidents in beery nights out, being fined by the Dean (I wish we had more than the tiny but exact glimpse near the start of 'Dockery and Son'). Nor did he go in for the sherry-sipping, exclusive-dinner side of Oxford—not that there can have been much of it in 1941–2 (the four terms he and I overlapped). The solitary creature of later years, unable to get through the day without spending a good part of it by himself, let alone the author of (say) 'First Sight', was invisible to me; most likely I was not looking hard enough.

If syllabus-literature was to be avoided wherever possible, writers beyond its scope could be all right, though of course not as exciting and discussable as Pee Wee Russell or Jack Teagarden.

Philip quickened my interest in or even introduced me to the work of Auden (above all), Isherwood, Betjeman, Anthony Powell, Montherlant (a lonely foreigner) and Henry Green, to *The Rock Pool* (Connolly), *At Swim-Two-Birds* (Flann O'Brien) and *The Senior Commoner* (Julian Hall), a wonderful marsh-light of a novel whose influence in 1946 or so was to help to render unpublishable the predecessor of *Lucky Jim*.

Much to my envy, Philip had poems published in undergraduate magazines. I published two of them myself in the OU Labour Club *Bulletin*, which I edited for a term in 1942, and was censured for bourgeois obscurantism by the Committee. How odd—the poems were quite straightforward, said Philip, glossing with a pair of monosyllables the first two nouns in the line 'The steeples and the fanlights of a dream'. This remark reached an unaccustomed depth and seriousness in our conversations about the craft of poetry. In my experience, poets who are any good only discuss their work as a reaction to criticism or if they need advice on some technical point. Philip had had no criticism then and he has never needed advice on technical points.

In that year and a bit, Philip Larkin was not the leading Oxford poet; that position was held by Sidney Keyes or Michael Meyer or John Heath-Stubbs. When *Eight Oxford Poets*, edited by the first two, appeared in 1941, Philip was not represented; it now appears that Keyes, who may well have known that Philip considered him a third-rate personage, left him out with some deliberation. This was annoying, but no great matter, for at that stage of his life his main intention was to become a novelist. (It was I who had decided to be a poet.) Parts of *Jill* were already in existence; one part, the Willow Gables fantasy, had come to independent life as a kind of pastiche of schoolgirl stories. When the book finally appeared I was amazed at the skill that half concealed the utter incongruity of that episode with the rest of the material. Well, perhaps in a way it was not so incongruous; certainly all the John Kemp parts showed me a Philip I had never known before.

I read, with permission, the early pages and even made suggestions. One of them got 'Cold it looked, cold and deserted' changed to 'It looked cold and deserted'. I saw little of *A Girl in Winter* before publication, but was consulted in some detail over Philip's third novel, a serio-comic account of the gradual involvement of a rising young executive in the motor industry, Sam Wagstaff, with a working-class girl he knocks down in his car coming home from the factory. Why this promising idea was abandoned, why its more ambitious successor went the same way, is obscure to me, but I suspect, alongside much else, the workings of that underrated agency in human affairs, fear of failure. No poem of Philip's preferred length lays your head on the block in the way any novel does.

This takes us to the later forties and the fifties, when I got to know Philip better than I ever had at Oxford; there, I had usually seen him as one of a group. In 1946 or so I went and stayed with him at his parents' house in Warwick. My chief memory of that visit is reading a manuscript, or rather typescript, book of his early, unpublished poems. A page near the front said,

The present edition is limited to 1 copy.
This is no. 1

(Anybody else I know would at least have taken carbons to give his chums.) The poems, written I suppose in his middle teens, evoked Auden, though not at all directly. It was uncomfortably clear to me that every one of them was better than any that I, aged twenty-four, had written. By then, of course, he had published *The North Ship*, and I had been quite sufficiently impressed by that but, perhaps oddly, it was these poems that he had never published that told me how good he was and would be.

In 1948 or so I went and stayed with him at his digs in Leicester. There he was in a house smelling of liniment, with a landlady who resembled a battered old squirrel and a dough-faced physicist co-lodger. On the Saturday morning he had to go into college and took me ('hope you won't mind—they're all right really') to the common-room for a quick coffee. I looked round a couple of times and said to myself, 'Christ; somebody ought to do some-

On holiday with his parents, 1939

Outside Bruce Montgomery's lodgings, 47 Wellington Square, Oxford (taken by Bruce Montgomery, 1943)

In his first office at Hull, 1956

With George Hartley at the back of 253, Hull Road, Hessle – first home of the Marvell Press – 1971

thing with this.' Not that it was awful—well, only a bit; it was strange and sort of *developed*, a whole mode of existence no one had got on to, like the SS in 1940, say. I would do something with it.

Jim Dixon's surname has something to do with ordinariness, but at the outset had much more to do with Dixon Drive, the street where Philip lived. Yes, for a short time it was to be his story. The fact that, as it turned out, Dixon resembles Larkin in not the smallest particular witnesses to the transmuting power of art. Philip came into *Lucky Jim* in quite another way. In 1950 or so I sent him my sprawling first draft and got back what amounted to a synopsis of the first third of the structure and other things besides. He decimated the characters that, in carried-away style, I had poured into the tale without care for the plot: local magnate Sir George Wettling, cricket-loving Philip Orchard, vivacious American visitor Teddy Wilson. He helped me to make a proper start. And I never even bought him a lunch!—not then, anyway.

In 1976 or so he and I were in a taxi on our way to a drink in London. I said into a silence, without premeditation,

'What chance of the Nobel?'

'Oh, that's gone,' he said decisively. 'I thought they might be keeping it warm for a chap like me—you know, a chap who never *writes* anything or *does* anything or *says* anything. But now I find they've just given it to an Eyetie bugger who never *writes* anything or *does* anything or *says* anything. No, that's *gone*.'

After a pause, I asked, 'What about the Laureateship?'

'I dream about that sometimes,' he said in the same tone, '*and wake up screaming*. Nah, with any luck they'll pass me over.'

End of conversation. What made me laugh about it was that Philip had spoken altogether naturally. Few other people would have had the self-mastery to exclude from their manner any trace of facetiousness or other defensive reaction when running through those facts. Here was a small but telling example of the total honesty that marks both him and his work. I have never known him say anything he did not mean; when he tells you he feels something, you can be quite sure he does feel it—a priceless asset to a poet, and a poet of sensation at that. The same quality ensures that when he has nothing to say he says nothing, which helps him not to write any bad poems.

I am grateful for having known Philip Larkin for over forty years, not only because he is my favourite poet—well, next to Housman (must try to be honest too), but because he is Philip. Although his manner has quietened since those Oxford days, he still treats the world with jovial acerbity, belying the sober, triste style of his photographs—well, there are gloomy moments, at least they would be if they were not so funny, about the TUC or the state of jazz or having to pay bills, or death, of course. He is the most enlivening companion I have ever known and the best letter-writer; to this day a glimpse of the Hull postmark brings that familiar tiny tingle of excitement and optimism, like a reminder of youth.

A Proper Sport

ROBERT CONQUEST

When *New Verse* published an Auden number back in the thirties the most interesting contribution was one by Christopher Isherwood, a combination of personal and literary chat. I did not have Isherwood's piece in mind when writing what follows, but I now wish I could have modelled myself on it. One trouble is that Isherwood was closer to his subject both personally and as a literary collaborator; nor can I claim Isherwood's narrative skill. Still, something of the sort, at least filling in a few minor cracks in the impressive structure around me, seems my only plausible resort, even though I shall be covering only one side of Larkin, if that.

I met him in the lobby of the Strand Palace Hotel, some twenty-five years ago. I was at once attracted by his personality—mild in manner, deprecatingly humorous, tough as nails. He was on his way to holiday in Sark, in accordance with his principle of never leaving the British Isles (a commitment since broken by a very brief culture-award trip to Hamburg). He was convinced, as he once put it to me, that if he ventured abroad, within days he'd be on a stretcher going back up the gangplank, his yellow skin flapping on his bones. He was later tempted by the idea of a direct flight to New Orleans, where I would meet him and convey him to the historic jazz locations, but only tempted. . . . Meanwhile it was Sark and North Uist (romantic-sounding Western Isle which turned out to be flat as Holland and covered with tulip-fields—a normal example of Larkin's Luck, to which I shall return). And Dorset, and Skye—of whose 'life-hostile gabbros' Auden writes, and of whose food Larkin now complained, provoking a limerick running, as far as I can reconstruct it from memory:

> Said Philip, least fussy of fabbros,
> 'They sure are life-hostile, these gabbros.
> There's nothing to eat
> But purée of peat
> With fried herring-bollocks and dab-roes.'

But for all that, preferable to Abroad. And of course Larkin's revulsion from the foreign is central to his poetry too. In one printed interview he was asked 'Do you read much foreign poetry?' and answered in a form printed, '*Foreign* poetry? No.' Once when some critic had pontificated, 'Mr Larkin must read Laforgue,' he wrote me, with extravagant insularity, 'If that chap Laforgue wants me to read him he'd better start writing in English.'

Of course the critic was wrong. This insularity is one of the strengths of Larkin's poetry, signifying a resolve to base himself firmly upon the experience, the language, the culture which have formed him, in which he is rooted. It was chiefly of Larkin that I was thinking when I wrote in the Introduction to *New Lines II*:

> . . . influences cannot just be meaningfully absorbed by an effort of will. It is equally true that the human condition from which the poetry of one country springs cannot be readily tapped by that of another. The British culture . . . is part of our experience, and for that no one else's experience, however desirable, can be a substitute.

I noted, too, that a true appreciation of French poetry in particular is very rare in Britain.

This first meeting with Larkin arose out of correspondence we had had in connection with the original *New Lines*. (The selection of poems for that anthology was complete before *The Less Deceived* came out: indeed, I fancy that for some of Larkin's, *New Lines* would have been the first appearance, but for the fact that its publication processes were much the slower.)

The draft introduction to *New Lines* was sent to all the contributors. I remember that while Kingsley Amis wanted it tougher,
Larkin would have preferred it milder. Certainly, it was not a
balanced or judicious piece. Nor was it intended to be—it was a
provocative showing of the flag, or trailing of the coat. In this it
succeeded: at any rate the collection attracted a remarkable
volume of abuse and some equally noisy championship—and
Larkin's private comments on some of the hostile critics were as
harsh as, and even coarser than, Amis's.

In the original draft of this introduction, the poetic perversities
attacked had included, and by name, the 'Movement', a word then
used to signify cerebral sub-Empsonian work like that of Al
Alvarez. I can't remember why this sentence was dropped:
presumably because some of the Wain and Amis poems were in
that mode—though included in spite of, rather than because of,
this. I wish, all the same, that I'd kept it in: it could, or might,
have spared us all the brouhaha about *New Lines* and the Movement which still goes on. To be fair to myself, I did say in that
introduction that all we had in common was no more than a wish
to avoid certain bad principles. As Thom Gunn put it later, all we
shared was what had been the practice of all English poets from
Chaucer to Hardy.

From this time on I saw a fair amount of Larkin. Sometimes he
stayed with us, though I only once managed to stay with him in
Hull, in his old Pearson Park flat—not such a gloomy hole as
some might envisage, being formerly that of the American consul.
We have held a continuous correspondence, especially in the
years I have meanwhile spent abroad. Among his earliest letters I
recall a series of sardonic comments on an astonishing cycle of
strokes of Larkin's Luck in publication and criticism, occurring
over a very short period: George Fraser, in his anthology *Poetry
Now*, listed Larkin as the second example in the category of
'regional' poetry, the first being the Lallans lot, and Larkin
featuring as a 'Northern Ireland regional poet': Larkin was then
working in Belfast, and this together with his sharing the name
of the well-known nationalist doubtless misled Fraser. Then in

New Lines, a misprint of the last word of stanza 7 line 2 of 'Church Going' made it 'rest' instead of 'meet', and in spite of efforts to correct this as each edition appeared, it always turned up un-abated. Not that anyone noticed. Meanwhile, he had appeared on the jacket of D. J. Enright's *Poets of the 1950s* as 'Larkins'. After that two well-known critics writing in serious journals missed points: one suggested that, in 'Toads', to say 'the stuff /That dreams are made on', instead of 'made of', just for the sake of a rhyme with 'pension', was a strained effect: the other (even more distinguished) noted as typical of Larkin's style the phrase 'A sweet girl-graduate'. These two cases show, incidentally, that Larkin was by no means as rigorous in avoiding quotation from others as might be thought to follow from his deprecation, in *Poets of the 1950s*, of 'casual allusions in poems to other poems or poets'.

Tennyson's 'sweet girl-graduate' does fit into Larkin, the poet of sentiment rather than romance, of chat or lyric rather than rhetoric, of pathos rather than tragedy. No doubt these themes have been pursued elsewhere in this volume, and I would prefer to look at something else, though it is not unrelated to such matters. Morley writes of Burke, 'As is usual with a man who has no true humour, Burke is also without true pathos'. Larkin's humour is part, a necessary part, of the mix: and it is to be sought not so much in the overtly humorous poems as in the personality behind, beside or beyond all the poems. I recall, from letters, two instances of Larkin's characteristic tone. When Kingsley Amis, reviewing a book of verse of which Larkin disapproved, wrote, 'This volume brought tears to my eyes', Larkin commented, 'Must have hit himself over the bridge of the nose with it, eh?' On a similar deflating note, he wrote me, of a mutual acquaint-ance's newly published life-story, 'The trouble with X writing an autobiography is that nothing interesting has ever happened to him.'

He is not pompous about his own work; at any rate is prepared for levity from those he knows appreciate it really. He has long since become used to condensations of or commentaries on his poems in limerick form. I can't remember the one on 'Dockery and Son'—I'm not even sure it was in limerick form—but at any rate it was a four- or five-line verse giving Dockery's reply, to the effect that he had had no intention of being 'added to', but was merely the victim of a faulty contraceptive. The latest, anyhow, was this version of 'Aubade':

> When Philip gets pissed off with death
> He turns all prophetic and saith,
> 'Fuck death, and fuck dying,
> The Cosmos ain't trying
> —And Christ all this gin on my breath!'

He seemed to appreciate this; and could anyhow hardly object in principle, since he had himself collaborated in a limerick version of verses by another poet friend. There was also talk, more appropriately, of a Blues version—the first line coming in perfectly, perhaps the sign of a real 'influence'. (Incidentally, has anyone noticed a certain resemblance in structure and rhetorical stress to *The City of Dreadful Night*? 'The anaesthetic from which none come round' is a truly Thomsonian verse-ending, for example.) As to the coarseness of language, I recall him sending me an uncompleted limerick when I was resident poet at the University of Buffalo, about a rather tiresome mutual acquaintance (stylistically and socially resembling the start of 'Vers de Société'):

> So you met old X Y when in Buffalo?
> You must often have wanted to stuff a loa-
> ded gun up his arse
> And not let him pass
> With no sterner rebuke than a gruff 'Hullo!'

The last two lines were added (by me) many years later, for tidiness' sake.

But coarseness of language is anyhow visible in the poems. A thesis on 'The Four-letter Word in Larkin' would cover, on a rough count, eight of these, several used more than once (plus a couple of dubious five-letter words). Sometimes they are used simply out of high spirits, as with the reckless alliteration of 'The

shit in the shuttered chateau'. The coarseness of 'The Card-
Players', on the other hand, is the true texture of 'The secret
bestial peace' of the poem. And the 'Groping back to bed after a
piss' in 'Sad Steps' is a true fulfilment of the often proclaimed but
so seldom realized 'bringing back to natural use' of the long
ostracized words—funny that even now such a success should be
so strikingly unusual (but perhaps it is beneficial both linguistically
and socially to have a pool of words under ban . . .). I find 'fuck'
in 'High Windows' less convincing, though it is hard to suggest
what else he might have said. 'Fart', in 'Posterity', has been
described to me by a shrewd American as the one dubious note
—though not of course for its coarseness—in an otherwise perfectly phrased bit of Acadamerican. The biggest fuss, of course, has
been over 'Books are a load of crap' at the end of 'A Study of
Reading Habits', but I have never seen any force in the objections.
As so often with poetry and fiction, the sentiment has been
directly charged to Larkin personally, which would indeed have
been doubly treasonable in a poet-librarian.

But anything approaching irony always runs into this trouble.
Larkin has had an even more absurd example of it in connection
with 'Naturally the Foundation Will Bear Your Expenses'. The
late Tom Driberg wrote a letter to the *New Statesman* heartily
agreeing with Larkin about his supposed attack on ceremonies for
the war dead and saying how he sympathized with the sneer at
'wreath-rubbish in Whitehall'. Of course the poem is in fact a
very hostile caricature of this smug anti-patriotism. How could
even Driberg imagine otherwise? He seems to have been blinkered
by the assumptions of the lumpenintelligentsia that all above a
minimal level of education, sensitivity, creativity and so on must
be lowest-common-factor lefties. At any rate, Larkin's political
views (though one should stress that this applies in matters far
beyond the purely political) are on the traditional far right.

A caricature of him, roneoed by a student group, shows his
oval, bespectacled head as the body of an octopus, with tentacles
covered with swastikas. But this was in protest at his actions, as a
librarian, in devising schemes to prevent the stealing of books,

though there was the occasion when he told the local student protest leader (who had won fame by refusing to take his exams) that
he could only win real respect by setting fire to himself. At any rate
the student editor was closer than Driberg, in the sense of showing
Larkin as a man of the Right—though not, indeed, of the radical
position (as 'left' as it was 'right') of the swastika swine.

No, he is a 'reactionary' in the broadest sense: for example
wanting to 'put the clock back' on 'development' and the ruin of
rural—or rather, in a larger way, traditional—England: a sentiment also to be found in the conservatism of Peter Simple.
'MCMXIV' and 'Homage to a Government' show this preference for the past to some degree; and his quatrain 'When the
Russian tanks roll westwards . . .' expresses his distaste at the
news that for the first time British expenditure on education had
exceeded that on defence.

But his views on politics are, of course, matched by 'reactionary' opinions on art and other matters. These are most forth-
rightly expressed in the introduction to *All What Jazz*, that most
devastating and direct assault on 'modernism'. Indeed, it is a pity,
not only from the point of view of establishing his outlook, that
this and other introductions, together with odd prose pieces to be
found in hard-to-get magazines like *Mabon* and *Umbrella*, have
not yet been collected. They would suitably supplement and (at
least to some slight extent) clarify the drift of the poetry.

There are various ways in which light may be thrown on such
a poetical personality. When (as Larkin himself notes of Betjeman)
critical and psychological rigours are hard, even impossible, to
achieve, the impressionistic and anecdotal may, I hope, contribute
exceptionally to a definition.

Publishing Larkin

CHARLES MONTEITH

'You remind me', Philip said, slowing to fifteen miles an hour and giving me a severe glance, 'of a Catholic priest, wondering why little ones aren't making regular appearances.' It was somewhere between Hull and Beverley, sometime between *The Whitsun Weddings* and *High Windows*. I had asked if there was any possibility of my seeing a new collection of poems within the next year or two. During the long and immensely enjoyable experience of being Philip's publisher such mortifying moments have, happily, been rare.

When I joined Faber & Faber in the early fifties I burned, as most young editors do, with an ambition to liven up the fiction list, and a number of people commended to my attention *A Girl in Winter*, a novel Faber had published in 1947. It was outstanding, its admirers said; and when I read it I agreed. What was happening? they asked. Why had there been no successor? Who is Philip Larkin? These questions sent me to the files and to the book's editor, Alan Pringle (who died in 1977).

It had arrived in May 1946, accompanied by one of those letters, all old-world formality and punctilio, which in those days accompanied submissions by A. P. Watt and Son. Terms were agreed; an exchange of correspondence followed between Russell Square and the Public Library, Wellington, Shropshire; the title was changed from *The Kingdom of Winter* to *A Girl in Winter* (Philip's own suggestion). The book was published in 1947, was well reviewed and sold—the war-time book-boom had not yet exhausted itself—nearly 5,000 copies.

Alan Pringle was, of course, delighted and began to enquire about its successor. Philip at first gave him guarded encouragement—'I have made an infinitely tentative start on another book' (1947), 'The novel becomes clearer to me in conception as time to work on it becomes shorter' (1948)—but by 1950 nothing had appeared, so Alan wrote again. To this the reply, dated 26 February 1950, was apologetic, pessimistic and conclusive. 'I am afraid that the answer is simply that I have been trying to write novels and failing either to finish them or to make them worth finishing. . . . I am beginning to think of the creative imagination as a fruit-machine on which victories are rare and separated by much vain expense; and represent a rare alignment of mental and spiritual qualities that normally are quite at odds.' That seemed to be that.

Nothing more happened until 1953 when I blundered enthusiastically on to the scene. Just as I was about to write I discovered that Philip and I had a friend in common who came, as I did, from Belfast where Philip was by then University Sub-librarian. My enthusiasm and eager enquiries were conveyed and responded to promptly, courteously but firmly. 'My last word to your encouraging firm on the subject of novel writing was a letter to Alan Pringle dated 26 February 1950 which should still be on file: I'm afraid it is still the case. We did meet, you know,' he added, 'in All Souls, but doubtless you've forgotten.'

It came back to me: the light of evening, Hawksmoor's towers, great windows open to the west. A literary party with lions loose in the throng: Kingsley Amis, for example, fresh from the publication of *Lucky Jim*, and Bruce Montgomery, whom I had only recently discovered to be 'Edmund Crispin'. Among the others was a quiet, spectacled, tall, balding young man—Larkin, I now realized—with whom I had a pleasant coversation by the gas-fire.

In my reply to Philip's letter I said that I'd be happy to read the abandoned novels if he thought that might be a help, but the offer was firmly rejected. 'I've been thinking about the creative process a good deal', he wrote, 'since I last wrote to your firm; instead of a fruit-machine it now seems to me to be a very delicate balance between what has happened and what one likes to think of as happening, and its function is to restore the balance after inroads have been made on one by reality. So my trouble may be insufficient invasions by reality, whatever that is—unhappiness, I suppose.'

Philip's letter ended on a friendly and reassuring note: 'I am glad you wrote; it did much to dispel my conception of Faber's as a reproachful father-figure'—but it also made an enquiry, almost as an aside. 'I sometimes write poetry, and am submitting a selection (six or seven) to an undergraduate concern called the Fantasy Press. . . . This doesn't worry you, does it?' I assured him that it didn't—the option clause in *The Girl in Winter* contract referred only to novels—but it reminded me of a brief exchange of letters in the earlier file. In January 1948 he had submitted, through A. P. Watt, a collection of poems called *In the Grip of Light* (an unpromising title, I thought) and it was returned on 3 February. Though Eliot probably looked at it—usually he gave all poetry submissions at least a glance—there was no note by him in the file.

There is nothing more in my own files until 1955, when I received a form from the Marvell Press of Hull—whom I connected with the admirable poetry magazine *Listen*—inviting me to subscribe to a volume called *The Less Deceived*; and I am happy to record that I did. It was only about then that I first became aware that Philip was a serious poet. I had read 'Church Going' in the *Spectator* before *The Less Deceived* appeared and had written to say how much I had liked it; *The Less Deceived* when it arrived (it was published later in 1955) produced more enthusiasm, and I passed it to Eliot who made a benign comment on the margin of my note to him: 'Yes—he often makes words do what he wants. Certainly worth encouraging.' In my letter I asked Philip if Faber could consider his next collection and he responded as I hoped he would: 'I'll remember your very exciting suggestion about F & F when I have another collection—about 1965 I expect! F & F has always been my ideal for poetry naturally.'

As we shall see, his prediction about the date of his next volume erred very slightly on the side of pessimism. During the intervening years our correspondence, far from declining in volume, became more frequent, more friendly and more personal. We met fairly regularly—as we still do—in London (on one of his visits to the Lords Test, to meetings of the Arts Council Manuscripts Committee, or board meetings of the Poetry Book Society of which he eventually became Chairman), in Hull (where I stayed as his guest in the gloomily splendid Station Hotel) or in Oxford (where he stayed with me in All Souls—a College where he later stayed in his own right as a Visiting Fellow and stays now as a member of Common Room).

In the summer postcards arrived, and continue to arrive, from remote corners of the United Kingdom. (As is well known, he concurs completely with George V's views on Abroad. Once, in a letter thanking me for a lunch at which I had persuaded him, against his better judgement, to eat a Greek meal, he described Retsina as 'that interesting wine which tastes of cricket bats'.) A postcard from Scotland, a colour photograph of a fox meaningfully eyeing a partridge, and on the reverse: 'Do you like this picture of a British author and H M Inspector of Taxes?'; from the Lake District, with a picture of a climber swaying dizzily on a rock face, 'A quiet week mostly spent doing *The Times* Crossword. This picture might be called The Ascent of F6 Across'; from Jura, 'George Orwell lived on this island for a bit and I guess this was his view. I imagine it hastened his end'; from Ullswater, 'Water-skiing seems to be the thing here—non nobis, Domine.'

By this time a current theme had made itself apparent in our correspondence—a series of persistent and somewhat thick-skinned enquiries by me about this next collection of poems. (He was free by now of any option obligation to the Marvell Press.) 'It is wonderful', he wrote to me in 1962, 'to have your occasional enquiries about a new book. They seem like enquiries from God as to how soon I can take up my post as seventy-first harpist. But . . . I should really rather wait . . . what I should like to do is write three or four stronger poems to give the whole thing some weight.' He confirmed later that he had broken the news to George Hartley (of the Marvell Press) that the next collection would be offered to Faber; and in June 1963 *The Whitsun Weddings* arrived.

Its critical reception was all that I had hoped for; a first printing of 4,000 was soon exhausted and a reprint was ordered shortly after publication. Some unexpected consequences followed too: 'An awful thing—a Professor Lal has written to me from Calcutta highly delighted at my mentioning him in that poem. He sends his own stuff. He runs something called Writers' Workshop. Am I fated to be *his* contact and *his* pal?' There was a television programme in Jonathan Miller's *Monitor* series; a graduate student at the North Dakota State University of Agriculture and Applied Science wrote a thesis on Philip's work 'in partial fulfilment of the requirements for the degree of Master of Arts'; the Queen's Gold Medal for Poetry arrived by post.

Other themes began to emerge in our correspondence, one of them the novels of Barbara Pym. Philip, for years a staunch admirer, had mentioned her before; and on Cape's refusal of her latest book in 1965, he steered it firmly in my direction. I enjoyed it, but only mildly—a feeling shared by its other readers in Faber & Faber—and I felt none of the inner excitement a publisher should feel when deciding to take on a new author. We were all, too, inclined to be pessimistic about the number of copies we would sell, if we were to publish it. Philip's disappointment was eloquent and heartfelt: 'I feel it is a great shame if ordinary sane novels about ordinary sane people doing ordinary sane things can't find a publisher these days. This is the tradition of Jane Austen and Trollope, and I refuse to believe that no one wants its successors today. Why should I have to choose between spy rubbish, science fiction rubbish, Negro-homosexual rubbish, or dope-taking nervous-break-down rubbish? I like to read about people who have done nothing spectacular, who aren't beautiful and lucky, who try to behave well in the limited field of activity they command, but who can see, in little autumnal moments of vision, that the so called "big" experiences of life are going to

miss them; and I like to read about such things presented not with
self pity or despair or romanticism, but with realistic firmness and
even humour. That is in fact what the critics call the moral tone
of the book. It seems to me the kind of writing a responsible
publisher ought to support (that's you, Charles!).' I explained my
reasons again and Philip replied, pacific but unconvinced: 'In all
her writing I find a continual perceptive attention to detail which
is a joy, and a steady background of rueful yet courageous
acceptance of things which I think more relevant to life as most
of us have to live it, than spies coming in from the cold. I think
"development" is a bit of a myth; lots of writers don't develop,
such as Thomas Hardy or P. G. Wodehouse, nor do we want
them to. That is how I feel about Miss Pym!' Recently I read, or
in some cases reread, half a dozen of Barbara Pym's novels, including all the later ones; and I realize, sadly but clearly, that in
1965 I made a mistake.

Another topic we corresponded about at length was the
republication of *The North Ship*. At first Philip was hesitant:
'They [the poems] are such complete rubbish, for the most part,
that I am just twice as unwilling to have two editions in print as
I am to have one.' The Fortune Press, however, which had first
published the book in 1945, continued to advertise and sell a
reprint which bore no indication to the purchaser that it was not
a genuine first edition; and this, more than anything, diminished
Philip's reluctance. Our lawyers advised us that we could safely
go ahead if we wanted to; and so we did, with Philip's approval.
He enjoyed, I think, writing the introduction which gives a
detailed account, both entertaining and scathing, of the book's
first publication. On the appearance of the Faber edition there
was not the slightest murmur of protest from R. A. Caton, the
proprietor of the Fortune Press. Philip had earlier rejected out of
hand a suggestion of mine that he should include in this volume
those poems in *XX Poems*—a privately printed collection, limited
to 100 copies, which he had published in Belfast in 1951—which
had not been subsequently included in *The Less Deceived*. 'I . . .
tried very hard to find it in my heart to agree with you. Unfortun-

ately I cannot rid myself of the conviction of what I should say about any of my contemporaries who published a collection along these lines. It would be (if my secretary can bear to type it): "Now the bastard has made himself a name he reckons he can unload any old crap", and if at the same time I should happen to be a reviewer I should make this view very plain.' My own copy of *XX Poems* is inscribed, 'To Charles, most efficient of friends and kindest of publishers'—which I find faintly worrying.

I had enquired, too, in 1966, if he was following events in Oxford, where Blunden and Lowell were the main contenders for the Chair of Poetry. (Blunden, to my surprise and disappointment, won a landslide victory.) 'I am really not in sympathy with the event,' he wrote. 'Surely I am right in thinking that the Chair was originally instituted to try to get some work out of the dons? *That* is a wonderful idea and one which I would heartily subscribe to. The present convention seems to me regrettably like electing a cow to a chair at an institute of dairying.'

In 1973, when Blunden's successor Roy Fuller had almost come to the end of his term of office (Blunden had retired early on grounds of ill health), Auden asked me, over dinner at Christ Church, if Philip could be persuaded to stand; and promised his fullest support if he did. Philip's reply was predictable: 'Your letter about the Chair of Poetry was immensely flattering. To know that Auden is willing to nominate me is the biggest compliment I have been paid for many years. I only wish I felt his confidence was justified, or could do something to justify it. But as you well know—and you do know me a good deal better than Auden does —I have really very little interest in poetry in the abstract; I have never lectured about it, or even written about it to any extent, and I know that I could never produce anything worthy of such a distinguished office and audience. The effort of trying to do so, moreover, would make my life hell for five years, and almost certainly stop me writing anything else, which would be (at least in my view) a disadvantage.'

About *All What Jazz*, his next book, he professed even greater pre-publication gloom than usual. 'I think the best line you can take', he wrote, 'is that you are promoting a freak publication: please don't put it forward as a piece of jazz scholarship or even as any sort of contribution to the field. Treat it like a book by T. S. Eliot on all-in-wrestling.' Despite this modesty, I approached him soon afterwards for advice when we were thinking about commissioning a life of Louis Armstrong. My enquiry produced two foolscap pages of combined erudition and enthusiasm. 'It is already accepted—or if it isn't it soon will be—that Louis Armstrong was an enormously important cultural figure in our century, more important than Picasso in my opinion but certainly quite comparable in stature. . . .' The letter proceeded with much pertinent and well-informed advice but the idea, alas, never came to anything, either because someone else was already at work on such a book or because we were unable to secure the collaboration of a suitable American publisher.

In 1972 and 1973 I thought I had detected the first signs of a new collection in the offing—most notably 'The Building' in the *New Statesman* and 'The Old Fools' in the *Listener*—and at the beginning of June 1973 *High Windows* arrived. Soon we were planning a reading on publication day, though not, of course, by Philip, who remained adamant in his refusal to perform in public. He hesitated about giving his blessing: 'I am not keen on poetry readings . . . I think they belong to the *demi-monde* of poetry. If you held one, it would be difficult for me not to attend it, and I am inclined to think that, unless one is extremely impressive in the flesh (like Bernard Shaw or Rupert Brooke), one gets more dividends from keeping out of sight, as people's imaginary picture of you is always so much more flattering than the reality. Nor do I think that new poems—unfamiliar poems—reap the full benefit of public reading, as people don't know them and find it hard to follow them.'

Despite these misgivings the reading was highly successful, though unfortunately Philip at the last moment was unable to come. The book's reception by the critics ensured—for us it was a record for a volume of new verse—that we sold out a first printing of 6,000 in three weeks. Since *High Windows* appeared

Philip's fame has grown steadily, a fact witnessed not only by the increasing number of critical studies of his work but also by such straws in the wind as a woman advertising in the *New Statesman* for a 'helpmate' who confided that she was a lover of 'trees, tarns and the latest Larkin', and the quotation in the 1976 edition of *The International Sex Maniac's Diary* of the first three lines of 'Annus Mirabilis'. (The editor of this publication, a Miss Tuppy Owen, BSc, sent Philip an aspidistra with a note saying that since his 'stuffy publishers' might not pass on the fee they had extracted she felt he should have this instead. The plant continues to flourish in Hull where it is known as The Owen Bequest.)

Our correspondence continues as enjoyably and regularly as ever. Fairly recently it included, on the back of a postcard showing a kilted Scot tossing the caber, The Second Faber Limerick:

> I hope games like tossing the caber
> Are never indulged in at Faber;
> To balance a column
> Of cash is more solemn
> And much more rewarding a labour!

The First Faber Limerick, written years before, was inspired by his chance passing though a village in North Yorkshire called Kaber which, he realized, provided the perfect rhyme. (I have a photograph of him draped glumly over the name-board.)

> There was an old fellow of Kaber,
> Who published a volume with Faber:
> When they said 'Join the club?'
> He ran off to the pub—
> But Charles called, 'You must *love* your neighbour.'

The somewhat obscure third and fourth lines Philip explained as 'fillers' to be replaced more specifically as occasion demanded. For example:

> When they said 'Meet Ted Hughes',
> He replied, 'I refuse',

or

> When they said, 'Meet Thom Gunn',
> He cried, 'God, I must run',

and so on.

And next? Time will show. I know better now than to ask when a new collection is likely to arrive.

Larkin the Librarian

B. C. BLOOMFIELD

By his own account Philip Larkin became a librarian largely through chance—and the wish to avoid the Minister of Labour's having to exercise upon him the powers of direction. Impercipient critics often appear to have difficulty in reconciling the popular stereotype of a librarian (thorough, pedantic, myopic and perpetually whispering 'Hush') with the more robust romantic image of a poet (shock-headed, open-shirted and tanned, tossing off lyrics and bastards indiscriminately); in the popular imagination Philip Larkin has settled somewhat uneasily between the two. But while his fame as a poet is generally diffused it is only a part-time job; what occupies the majority of his waking hours is the business of running an efficient and effective library to serve the academic community, teaching staff and students, of an English provincial university—Hull. This is an attempt to set out the background to Philip Larkin's particular 'toad', librarianship.

Having come down from Oxford in summer 1943 with a first class degree in English, Philip Larkin was living at home writing a novel when the Minister of Labour wrote asking what contribution he was making to the war effort. (Unfit for military service, he could have been directed to any job deemed suitable.) On the day that the letter arrived the *Birmingham Post* contained an advertisement for the post of Librarian in the Public Library at Wellington; Philip applied, was interviewed and, without any training or experience except that gleaned from habitual use of libraries, was appointed to succeed the previous incumbent— appointed in 1903! He was responsible almost single-handed for

48

running the library; there were lending and children's depart-
ments, some reference books, and the hours were long. In
addition there were the tasks of reporting to the Library Committee and stoking the boiler. At that time new books were
difficult to obtain on account of the paper shortage and money
to purchase was almost scarcer. Yet Philip soon took a grip of his
first job, sorted out what usable books there were, appealed for
and obtained new stock, joined the national inter-lending system,
imported extra stock from the County Library on loan and began
a series of quarterly reports to the Library Committee typed on his
own typewriter and mimeographed. The first report, dated
January 1944, summarizes a desperate position fairly, and subsequent reports record a continuing struggle to improve the
service to members of the library. An assistant was appointed in
the middle of 1945 and reports after that date are signed 'Chief
Librarian'! The town of Wellington more than got its money from
the new Librarian but was slow to provide facilities to ease his
lot. (He continued to use his own typewriter almost until he
resigned and one of his reports contains a plea that the Library
Committee should authorize the purchase of a machine for
library use as the Librarian can no longer guarantee to use his
own for library purposes. It was no doubt at this time employed
on producing *A Girl in Winter*.) He resigned on appointment as
an Assistant Librarian at University College, Leicester.

Philip took up his new post on 9 September 1946. Here, with
the encouragement of the then Librarian, Miss Bennett, he studied
in his own spare time for the Associateship of the Library Association, passed the examinations and was elected in 1949. His duties
in the library included issuing books to readers and answering
their questions, reshelving returned books, cataloguing books
and writing out catalogue cards by hand. (He was again responsible for this library's purchasing its first typewriter.) It was the
general library of a small, friendly university college whose
degrees were regulated and awarded by the remote, impersonal
University of London. Philip played his full part in social and
academic activities and at a time of gradual growth helped the

49

new library to develop on sound lines while at the same time enlarging his professional library experience and qualifications.

On 1 October 1950 Philip was appointed one of two sub-librarians at Queen's University, Belfast, under Jack Graneek, then Librarian. His responsibility was for reader services and his office (later remodelled to become a porter's box) was minute but a centre of gossip and activity. (The Larkin–librarian's duffle-coat with mysteriously clinking pockets figures in recollections of this time.) Belfast was quite different from Leicester although both were small academic communities with close links between teachers, librarians and the taught, and, of course, all this was before the outbreak of serious political trouble in the province. Philip resigned this post on 31 March 1955 to take up the post of Librarian at the University of Hull which he still holds.

Here again Philip took over a library that had only one previous librarian: Miss Agnes Cuming had been appointed in 1920 when the University College was founded. Others will deal in greater detail with Philip's time at Hull but it is worth remembering that when he was appointed the library was tiny, with a stock of about 124,000 items, a staff of twelve and a grant of £4,500 to pay for all purchases of books, periodicals and binding. There were only 727 students, annual book loans of 32,370 and annual acquisitions of 3,985 items. Contrast this with the position in 1979 when there was a stock of 567,277 items, a staff of about ninety-two, a grant for purchases of £284,148, 5,189 students, annual loans of 267,435 and annual acquisitions of 26,640 items. All achieved in twenty-four years with the help and dedication of the staff and University, channelled and directed by a supremely successful librarian taking advantage of the favourable climate of expansion in university education provided by the Robbins report.

There are few British university libraries which have come so far so successfully in such a short time, and, in addition, Philip Larkin has pioneered new techniques and introduced methods which have been copied in other academic libraries in the United Kingdom. He has been responsible for the introduction of the University Photographic Service (1958–9); has persuaded the

University into one new library building (opened by Her Majesty The Queen Mother on 20 June 1960), and then another (1968–9); initiated and built up the University's publishing programme as Secretary of the Publications Committee from its beginning until 1979; has encouraged and built up distinguished national collections of manuscripts (Labour history—in conjunction with John Saville, Conrad Noel, the Co-operative Productive Federation, the papers of the National Council for Civil Liberties, the Socialist Medical Association, the Women's Co-operative Guild) and a number of literary figures (among them Stevie Smith, Douglas Dunn, who once worked in the Library, and Vernon Watkins); celebrated the Library's 50th anniversary with a pamphlet history; defended its integrity in a celebrated dispute over access which resulted in the Publishers' Association withdrawing the University's library licence in 1973; and in 1980 pioneered the introduction of a new computerized and automated circulation system from Canada. The research collections of the new University of Hull are worthy of a university and play a full part in its academic life.

All this has been achieved by a dedicated professional librarian who at the same time has been one of the most distinguished figures on the campus, and by his renown as a poet, novelist, anthologist and critic has attracted students to the University and donations to the Library. He has also been responsible for introducing extended reading facilities for students, a poetry room and collection on the model of that at Harvard, a poetry lectureship now sadly suspended, and an Albion press for practical printing. In all these activities he has brought renown to British university librarianship and his colleagues, by an unremitting and particular attention to quality and detail to which his staff will testify.

And all the while he has managed to play a full part in other library activities. A member of the Standing Conference of National and University Libraries (SCONUL) representing his University, he has served on the Training and Education, Buildings, Publications and Inter-Library Loans Sub-Committees; and I still remember with delight the informal oral reports of the

Sub-Committee on Statistics which consisted of Philip Larkin and Geoffrey Woledge, then Librarian of the London School of Economics. Philip has also served on the Joint Committee with the former Association of British Orientalists and as alternate Chairman of the South East Asia Library Group, resigning after four years service in July 1975.

However, I suppose his best known library activity has been his Chairmanship of the Arts Council Committee on the National Manuscript Collection of Contemporary Writers. The first—and only—Chairman of this Committee, the idea of the collection and the provision of money to subsidize the purchase of such manuscripts by university and research libraries to try to ensure that important literary manuscripts remained in this country and were not all exported to the United States was entirely his. The fact that we still have any contemporary literary manuscripts in this country and that public opinion was roused, if ever so slightly, to this problem is in large part owing to his efforts.

In September 1979 the Library Association recognized his distinction as a librarian by awarding him its Honorary Fellowship at the combined conference in Sheffield. The applause of one's colleagues is always pleasant and in this case scarcely tinged by any literary prejudice, although Douglas Foskett, in making the citation speech, did quote:

> 'How many lives would have been duller
> Had he not been here below?'

A sentiment which will be applauded by his academic and library colleagues at the University of Hull, those students who have been fortunate enough to have studied at the University since 1955, and all his friends in libraries in the United Kingdom.

Note. Much of the information in this note is derived from printed sources recorded in my *Philip Larkin: a bibliography, 1933-1976* (London, Faber & Faber, 1979) especially items listed as C 127, C 172a, C 371, C 378, C 407, C 413, D 1-31, and H 16; I am indebted for additional help to Mr A. J. Loveday, Mr D. G. F. Walker, and Mr W. G. Wheeler.

Memoirs of the Brynmor Jones Library

DOUGLAS DUNN

About twenty years ago, on the first day of classes at the Scottish School of Librarianship, I was riveted by the definition of the job which some high-flying bookman had come up with. 'Librarianship', the lecturer plugged, as if trying to convince himself, 'is the handmaiden of the arts.' It seemed a pretentious claim to a slip of a lad who had just spent a year as a library assistant in Renfrew County Libraries. Part of my work involved standing in for holidaying or sick librarians, at village centres, or small branch libraries, in places with names like Uplawmoor, Inverkip, Langbank, Kilmacolm and Lochwinnoch. To save on bus-fares, I tripped around on a bike. Having, then, just finished a spell as a sub-literary cyclist—'special requests' and Auden's *Collected Shorter Poems* in my saddlebags—I felt as if I had been mistakenly metamorphosed into a tenth Muse, a 'handmaiden of the arts'. I took off my cycle-clips in awkward reverence.

Three libraries and three handmaidenships later, in the autumn of 1967, I turned up in Hull as an undergraduate in the English Department. I already knew, from my knowledge of the profession more than from any knowledge of contemporary verse, that the Librarian at Hull was Philip Larkin. Until a few weeks before, I had been tending the Joseph Black Chemistry Library at the University of Glasgow: it sounds impressive, but it wasn't, and I certainly wasn't. A senior librarian at Glasgow told me that, being a poet, Philip Larkin did not speak to simply anyone. 'He lives the life of the mind,' it was said. I had the feeling that some poor chap was being misrepresented. Imperfect conclusions about

Philip's personality are rife in literary criticism. When a poet is personal, or seemingly so, or self-deprecatory in his work, these false descriptions are practically invited: review the writer, not the writing. When he is a public figure, even in a community as self-contained as that of a university, or the profession of university librarianship, it is inevitable that other inmates of the same campus should be curious enough about him as to have an opinion. One excrescence of this habit of commenting upon campus 'characters' was to be seen in the gentlemen's lavatory at Hull (where it did not survive for very long). 'Knock three times,' it said on the door of a fuse-box, ten feet off the floor, 'and ask for Philip Larkin.' Who wrote it, and how did he get up *there*? Who else, I suppose, other than the eponymous Jake Balokowsky, refused an audience?

At twenty-four, married, and short of wherewithal, I needed paid work in my first long vacation. I applied to the Library and was appointed as a summer dogsbody in the Cataloguing Department. My boss was Brenda Moon, who is now Librarian at the University of Edinburgh. As Philip would be the first to confirm, much of the credit for the present excellence of the Brynmor Jones is due to Miss Moon's professional capacities.

In retrospect, that couple of months was the happiest, most exquisitely boring bout of librarianship I have ever undertaken. Much library work, at these less senior, more routine levels, is steady, gentle and undemanding. It gives you the illusion of leisure as the long summer days go by and no sweat breaks on the brow. I had already grown fond of the Library by using it. I love libraries and have a long list of favourites. The Brynmor Jones is at the top, closely followed by the Reference Room at Paisley Public Library, The Mitchell Library, Glasgow, and the old Andersonian Library in what used to be the Royal College of Science and Technology (especially the gallery which housed John Anderson's collection of books). A working familiarity with a library can lead to a peculiar fondness for such sights as a Reading Room at night, after the readers have gone home and the long tables gleam through the deep polish of many an elbow. You can grow to love particular corners of shelving, as the light changes its mood on dross and masterpieces alike. All books look strangely equal. To the professional beholder, they look 'processed' and pleasingly ordered. You can open a book and tell who catalogued it from the handwriting inside, someone, perhaps, who has moved on, or died. *Deeply* satisfying.

In the few brief conversations I had with Philip that summer—in the Catalogue Hall, in the cataloguing workshop as he passed through on some librarianly errand—the last subject I felt like raising was poetry: whether from fear, nervousness, or an overdose of respectful discretion on my part, I don't know. In any case, I was less interested in Philip's verse than in his management of discreet executive gifts on the one hand, a life of writing on the other. He was doing what I wanted to do, exactly. His presence encouraged me to believe that if he could get away with being a university librarian, and a poet, then so could I. As it turned out, the first was not my bag at all, no matter how much I thought it was at the time, and the second is probably in dispute. In spite of the conspicuous differences between us, I took him as my example of professional and literary decorum in, so to speak, action.

Then the rot set in. Or that is one of the ways I look at it. Certainly, poetry intervened. In the spring of 1968, I stopped to chat with Philip on the windy court between the Admin Block and the Faculty of Arts. Some months before, I had submitted an unpublished manuscript to the Society of Authors, to be considered for a Gregory Award. Unknown to me, Philip sat on its panel of assessors. As he broached this subject, I experienced, for the first time, his broad, wry, beaming smile. It was, and is, a token of serious amusement, with an engaging uplift and filling out of his cheeks, and an open-eyed invitation to say something for yourself. But the smile was one of encouragement and, though this is hindsight, it may also have been a warning of what I was letting myself in for. That wry grin, as I have seen it since, sometimes means, 'You should have known better,' or 'It serves you right.' Although Philip has been supportive of my own work—he helped me arrange *Terry Street*, and turfed out the more obvious duds—his encouragement is a bit like André Gide's. Camus, somewhere in his *Carnets*, I think, reports Gide talking about young novelists who sent him unpublished manuscripts, asking Gide if he thought they were good enough to continue writing. 'You mean,' Gide wrote back, 'you mean, you can stop, and you *hesitate*?'

After graduating, I was appointed as an acquisitions librarian in the Brynmor Jones—that is, I bought the books. Other than bibliographical nonsense in coat-hanger languages, perpetrated by a department of South-East Asian Studies (it had all but broken my predecessor, who took a rest-cure by moving next door to the Cataloguing Department) my chief headache was the Library's book budget. Handling new books is addictive, or would be, were it not for the avalanches of paperwork that accompany it. Day in, day out, invoices, order forms, catalogues, all seemed to be there to elicit the exposure of my innumeracy.

Among the many separate funds in the book budget, the Reserve Fund was the largest, a substantial sum set aside for the purchase of expensive but desirable books and sets, or back-runs of periodicals, these being the concern of Maeve Brennan, another of the efficient and dedicated librarians who have helped Philip make the Brynmor Jones the fine library it is. The Reserve Fund was supervised by a committee over which Philip presided with an elegant combination of good grace, bad grace, and sheer watchfulness. These are qualities which senior handmaidens of the arts acquire in due course if they do not have them to start with. 'Do we really need this?' Print is not subtle enough to portray the emphases which an ironic speaker like Philip can place in a sentence like that, as neatly, as magisterially, as omnipotently as one of Jane Austen's narrators. And that wry grin, with a slight lounge to one side, or a leaning back in his chair, would add the merest hint of impatience, just enough to start you worrying. Another characteristic committee-man's ploy of Philip's is a studied look at his pocket-watch, consulted in the palm of his hand as if he is holding a treasured irritant, a small mammal which might bite, not him, but you, if you waffle on much longer.

My immediate boss in the Brynmor Jones was the late Arthur Wood. He was a bookman, a plump, agreeable, ex-naval Glaswegian, and a connoisseur of Roxburghe Club Reprints, fine printings, bindings, and the catalogues of secondhand booksellers, which he read like novels. 'My goodness, Douglas,' he said one day, handing me a ten-year-old list, 'this was a *good* catalogue.' Looking it over, I saw he had pillaged it for a score of desiderata, including, inevitably, a couple of Roxburghes. Arthur was the opposite breed of librarian to Philip, who, after all, is the author of that offensive phrase, 'Books are a load of crap'. Not that Arthur was actually interested in what was *inside* these books, which, from the security of his desk, he sought for in the nation's antiquarian bookshops. For certain kinds of books you did not have to consult the catalogue to find out if we had a particular title in stock. In fact, Arthur liked to be asked, as if he understood why the catalogue was being by-passed: he loathed the catalogue, while, as an acquisitions man, he felt obliged to dislike cataloguers as well, ignoring them at every opportunity and saddened by the fact that the books we bought ended up on their desks. Asking Arthur 'Do we have this?' would bring forth statements of where it was bought, when, how much it cost, and how much cheaper that was than if we had bought it from so-and-so, some bookseller who was a notorious over-charger. On the other hand, I noted that Arthur's memory was far from infallible: we seemed to acquire an awful lot of duplicates. He also liked a proper lunch, soup, meat and two veg, and sticky pudding, eaten at a solid table with serious cutlery, in the dining-room of the old Senior Common Room, which looked the part, with its rustic but academic inelegance, overlooked by the undistinguished portrait of some learned gent. University carbohydrates were probably Arthur's undoing. He appears as Arnold in Philip's 'Self's the Man', and as himself in my own poem 'Christmas Refectory'.

By 1970, the Brynmor Jones was a different Library from the one I had known as a temporary factotum in 1967. It was bigger. During the time I was a student, a nine-storey extension had been built, and the rest of the building remodelled. In 1967 it had been given its name. All libraries ought to have names, and they ought to be called after benefactors who, like Sir Brynmor Jones, a Vice-Chancellor of the university, held the very proper conviction that good universities deserve good libraries. Hull's is a well named library. Fortunately, I missed the transference of books which these additions and alterations involved. I had endured one such flitting before, so I was not sad to miss another. When the Royal College of Science and Technology became the University of Strathclyde, much of the Library seemed to cross the road on my back.

Towards the end of the year, the young ladies who staffed my department said, on my birthday, that working for me was not too bad. It reminded me of Pee Wee Russell's idea of a compliment: 'It doesn't bother me.' It was well meant, and I was heartened. 'You're just like one of the girls, Douglas,' one said, followed by a collective of titters. Touched and terrified, pleased and panicking in the same moment, feeling sure that they did not mean it *literally*—or did they?—I rooted out Philip in his safe, spacious accommodation. He was either on the point of leaving for a sabbatical at All Souls in Oxford, or had come back for a few days of real work: at the time, he was trying to break the back of his *Oxford Book of Twentieth-Century English Verse*. A plaintive member of staff was probably what he wanted least, but it was what he got. My request was not outrageous, but, in context, it was unreasonable: I wanted an office, a small, very small one would do, and all it had to have were walls and a door.

From the first, I had admired how Philip held down a demanding job, and managed to write poems in that part of the day that is risibly called one's 'free time'. It was this second part of the equation I found myself unable to complete. Unlike teaching, librarianship brings with it no long vacations or easy-going timetable. I hankered after the life of a freelance writer, which Philip, if he has thought of it at all, may well look down on as a life of reprehensible shirking. He always claims that librarianship is a good job for a poet, and to some extent he is right. My problem was, that while I enjoyed my work—I still think of myself as a librarian, resting—I was making notes for writing, but finishing nothing. Arguments about lecturers who taught, and wrote, were pretty unconvincing as far as I was concerned: these swine had months and months of holidays in which, in my opinion, if they did not write, publish, or do something else constructive, then they ought to have been sacked forthwith. Accordingly, I put writing before income, resigned, and wrote, canvassing, no doubt, my eternal damnation. Philip greeted this change in my ambitions with his wry grin, his considering, avuncular stoop, with head-shaking, attempts at dissuasion, and, finally, his trump card, which was a loan of Cyril Connolly's *Enemies of Promise*, with that chapter on the career of Shelley-Blake conspicuously bookmarked for my convenience. It was meant to bring me to my senses, and sometimes (sometimes? often!) I wish that it had succeeded.

In the autumn of 1974 I went back to the Brynmor Jones as a Fellow in Creative Writing. I had an office, with a door, and I stood in it, savouring the irony. On that first day I went to see Philip, to prove to him that I could still get out of bed by nine a.m. After a few remarks along the lines of 'Now look at you. You should never have left Acquisitions', we talked about what was expected of a Fellow in Creative Writing. 'There's too much poetry on this campus,' he said. 'I'm relying on you to stamp it out. Come down *hard* on them!' Hazily understood as the duties of a Fellow in Creative Writing are, stamping poetry out— treading, indeed, the grapes of wrath—is unlikely to be accepted as one of them.

From recent published interviews, it may seem as if that callow, facetious and dismissive opinion of new poetry is typical of Philip's mind. And yet he is the poet of 'celestial recurrences', of 'unfenced existence', a poet whose lyrical sweep is broad as well as delicate and surprising. In some poems he is coarse and irascible, and sublimely lyrical and moving at the same time (or, at least, a few lines later). A sharp contrast of loveliness and colloquial vulgarity is a technique I associate with classic Scottish poetry. But Philip Larkin's writing is very English indeed, and his coarseness is English too, characteristically so. What he has done is write with the courage of his whole mind, giving us a slice of English sensibility, its crude laughter, its mock philistinism, as well as the tenderness, sadness, compassion and perception of beauty, of which, perhaps, only an English poet at his best is ever entirely capable.

Approaching the Brynmor Jones, before the hazard of its revolving doors, I always look up at Philip's office. It is on the second floor, immediately above the main entrance. Usually the gauze curtains are blowing through open windows. Inside is a librarian, an old colleague, and a friend, in whose good care, I know, all our books are safe, fastidiously filed and looked after by a staff who like their boss, the whole place ticking, populated, and busily alive. There is a lot to be said for being 'a handmaiden of the arts'. It curbs vainglorious thoughts and it teaches humility in its practitioners who are also authors. Philip thinks of his brochure *The Brynmor Jones Library 1929–1979* (University of Hull, 1979) as his 'last book'. I hope it is not, for if he feels he has no more poems he wants to write, he has a book about libraries in him, one which would be a fine addition to our professional literature.

On the border at Coldstream, 1962

Anthony Powell, Kingsley Amis, Philip Larkin and Hilary Amis after lunch in
London, 1958

With Monica Jones and others, waiting to receive the Shakespeare Prize 1976
(FVS Foundation Hamburg) in the Kaisersaal of the Hamburg City Hall

Meeting Philip Larkin

HARRY CHAMBERS

The first meeting, a carefully planned Porlockian invasion, happened in Hull one Saturday afternoon in September 1963. I hadn't discovered *The Less Deceived* until my second year at Liverpool University, four years after its first publication. My response then—an enormous and, possibly to the author, embarrassing 'Yes' not much this side of idolatry—hasn't developed much over the years.

There had been an exchange of letters following my Spring 1960 review of *The Less Deceived* in *Phoenix*, a magazine which I had founded in Liverpool, and another after one of my sixth-form students at a Grammar School near Doncaster had written about 'Essential Beauty' in the school magazine soon after its first appearance in the *Spectator*. (I was amazed recently to discover the school magazine article listed in the Bloomfield *Bibliography*.)

I told Philip Larkin that I had to travel the 'Here' route from Doncaster to Hull to pick up a second-hand Varietype machine, or some such flimsy pretext, and asked would a meeting be possible. Unwisely, he failed to reply that it wouldn't, so I proceeded in my attempt to hunt him down, taking with me for moral support a University friend, the poet David Selzer. We found the flat, in Pearson Park, rang the doorbell several times without getting any response, then took to trailing the various possible Larkins who were threading their pursed-up ways across the park. When all had been eliminated we returned to give the doorbell a few more rings before competing in inventing the most unlikely reason for the poet's apparent absence from home. Was he having a driving lesson? A dancing lesson even?

It was then that the afternoon sun revealed a flash of spectacles from an upstairs window. Shamelessly, we concluded that the doorbell couldn't be working, got ourselves let in by the occupant of the ground-floor flat and followed the sound of jazz upstairs to hammer on a door marked P. A. Larkin. The man who once wrote Eddie Condon a fan letter opened it, diagnosed both my condition and who I was and supposed that we had better come in. Looking back on it, I worked out that what we had interrupted was the writing of Larkin's jazz record review that was to appear in the *Daily Telegraph* of 9 October 1963.

I can't remember a great deal of what we talked about that afternoon—the copy of *The Less Deceived* that I took with me got inscribed 'gin/sausages/jazz'—but I seem to remember Philip confessing to having got into difficulties with a poem about dancing. Also I was most impressed by a montage in the bathroom juxtaposing Blake's 'Union of Body And Soul' with a Punch-type cartoon of the front and back legs of a pantomime horse pulling in opposite directions against one another and captioned 'Ah, at last I've found you!'. (It struck me later that this sort of caption has much in common with Larkin's technique of titling for a certain kind of poem, e.g. 'Annus Mirabilis', 'This Be The Verse', 'Self's The Man' and 'Naturally the Foundation Will Bear Your Expenses'; also that Our Old Friend Dualism seems to be a truthful enough gatekeeper to the world of Philip Larkin's poems.) That first meeting ended when Philip had to go out to play cards, whist, I think, with one of his secretaries who was convalescing after an operation. Philip offered us a lift part of the way to the station in the taxi that he had ordered. The taxi-driver was on Christian name terms with him.

The second meeting was more of a frail, travelling coincidence. On Sunday 1 March 1964 I was travelling by train from Liverpool to Doncaster and reading a pre-publication review copy of *The Whitsun Weddings*. At one of the Rotherham stations, Masborough perhaps, Philip Larkin boarded the train and sat in the first-class compartment immediately adjacent to my second-class one. It suddenly struck me that my review of *The Less Deceived* had said that 'the poetic landscape from his railway carriage (second-class compartment) is real and has not been seen for a long time.' But when I had recovered sufficiently from the shock to be able to wave *The Whitsun Weddings* at him, he beckoned me to join him and I nearly forgot to ask for my copy to be inscribed when I had to get out at Doncaster. I believe that it was soon after this meeting that he took driving lessons and bought a car. . . .

Our third meeting was in the mid-sixties in Belfast. (I had gone there in 1964 to lecture at a teacher training college, and Philip, I remember, had recommended me the walk along the Lagan as being the equal of anything in Oxford, and, he hoped, Doncaster.) He was re-visiting Belfast as a celebrity guest to the Bowra lectures and invited me to meet him in the staff bar at Queen's University. On a visit to the Gents—we were in adjacent stalls—I plucked up courage to confess that I was thinking of turning my interest in his poetry into thesis-fodder. The meeting was made memorable by his lugubrious reply: 'My God, Harry, you make me feel half-dead already! Why don't you choose someone else like, er, um . . . Ted Hughes?'

The foyer of the University Theatre, Manchester, was the scene of our fourth brief meeting, probably in the late sixties or early seventies. (I had moved from Belfast to a South Manchester College in 1967.) The occasion was the opening of Professor C. B. Cox's Manchester University Poetry Centre by W. H. Auden. (Auden read on the set of *Journey's End* and at one point nearly plunged to carpet-slippered doom after tripping over a parapet-limb.) I seem to remember Philip muttering that *he* would sooner be asked to open a leper colony.

There were two other meetings, both connected with the sale of the *Phoenix* archives—including several letters from Philip Larkin to myself, mainly, but not all, about the special Larkin issue of *Phoenix* (Nos. 11/12, Autumn and Winter 1973–4)—to the Library of Hull University. The Hull archivist, Norman Higson, had impressed upon me the need not to disturb what he called in all innocence the 'natural order' of the archive. Phildi himself drove over from Hull to my home at Heaton Mersey to collect the archive and have lunch. (It took Norman Higson over a year to sort out the chaotic contents of the various shoe-boxes and wallet files that Philip stowed in the boot of his car. I then went through to Hull University to combine some Larkin research with retrieving a few letters from widowed and maiden aunts that had crept somehow into the archive. Philip spent his lunch hour with me, regaled me with the tale of his Dolmen Press 'rejection-lunch' for *The Less Deceived* manuscript and very kindly drove me out to a bookshop called The White Rabbit at Beverley.) After lunch, Philip didn't exactly dandle my two-year-old daughter, Hannah, on his knee, but produced and swung for her delighted inspection a large fob-watch: a wonderfully Larkinian image and perhaps one intended to please me as much as my daughter. I mentally filed it as 'the infant Chambers standing under the fobbed Impendent belly of Time'. But I never did complete my thesis.

On the Plain of Holderness

ANDREW MOTION

Like most people, I had a favourite teacher. Mine was called Peter Way and I owe him, among many other things, my first sight of a poem by Philip Larkin. Until the age of sixteen or so I'd done very little except worry, play games and drift about. But when my 'A' level courses began, Mr Way set about turning me into a more constructive boy. His efforts included lending me a couple of books—one was Helen Thomas's *As It Was and World Without End* and the other was *The Less Deceived*. 'Dockery and Son' (cut out of a journal and faded yellow) was pasted inside the front cover, and although I had only a vague comprehension of it, I was immediately hooked. I read the book with the kind of excited absorption that only a handful of other poets have given me since. When a slightly younger boy, Anderson, let it be known that he was shortly to go into Oxford on a shopping expedition, I gave him a blank cheque and told him 'Buy all the Larkin you can find'. He came back with the two novels. The next week-end I went myself and got the (then only three) books of poems. 'February 1971', they say, in the repulsive turquoise ink I favoured at the time.

A few years later Mr Way's other loan paid off. After finishing my degree I started writing a thesis on the poetry of Edward Thomas. I liked Thomas very much (and still do), and I thought that coming to grips with him would increase my understanding of subsequent writers who have worked in the same tradition. Larkin was never very far from my mind—not simply because of occasional similarities in phrasing and cadence, but because there seemed to be certain resemblances between their sensibilities. Both are scrupulous, reserved, fastidious, fine-grained writers, acutely conscious of their position as isolated on-lookers, and preoccupied by the passage and ravages of time. And both articulate a sense of Englishness. It's a notoriously imprecise term, but among the members of what has been called this 'English line' would obviously be Cowper, Clare and Wordsworth. Many other names spring to mind (Housman, for instance), but even these few are enough to indicate an important branch of Larkin's poetic ancestry. They also prompt the reflection that his own work differs dramatically and in many ways from theirs—and in particular from Thomas's. For one thing, Larkin's language and rhythm are usually more robust. For another, the setting of his poems is more often urban, and where it isn't, the landscapes tend to be remote and flat, rather than secluding, sloping and southern.

For the last twenty-five years there's been one very good pragmatic reason why his landscapes should so often be as they are. In 1955 he moved to Hull, and it would be hard to find a well-populated area of England which was more geographically remote, or more spectacularly lacking in hills, than the Plain of Holderness. I found this out for myself in 1977 when I was appointed a lecturer in the English Department of the University of Hull. I was delighted to get the job—there weren't many around, I was keen to leave Oxford, and at last I had the chance, in theory anyway, to meet Larkin. 'High windows,' I said to one of my future professors after the interview, pointing towards the tall glassy library. 'Yes,' he said blankly—making me realize I was the umpteenth person to have said the identical thing that day.

Nevertheless, the same professor introduced me to Larkin a few days after the beginning of my first term. My initial impressions remain with me clearly. A taller, broader man than I'd imagined; dark-suited; a slight stammerer; reticent but leaning slightly forward; and immensely courteous. I didn't mention his poems at all, and nor did he mine. In fact I wasn't sure whether he knew I'd written any—or if he did, whether he thought them too worthless to mention. But before long our conversation was encouraged to take a more literary turn. The *Hull Daily Mail* asked us to judge a poetry competition to be entered only by local people writing on local subjects. It was called 'Bard of Humberside'—as if that accolade hadn't been given already. After reading through the entries we met to choose the winners. A couple of moments from that evening stand out in my memory. One is his leaning forward to stress the responsibilities that poets have to entertain their audience. 'Hit them with everything you've got— form, rhyme, variation of pace . . .' The second is his retelling a story from Hesketh Pearson's biography of Oscar Wilde, in which Wilde consoles a recently bereaved woman with enormous generosity. It was obviously an incident which Larkin admired deeply—and like the other memory it's probably stayed with me because it emphasizes a quality in his own poems. As often as they register the certainty of unsuccess, loneliness and death, they assert the value and resilience of human charity.

Since that evening we've met regularly. In all this time, he's only published one poem—'Aubade', in the *TLS*—most of which was written considerably earlier. At first, I imagined him to be producing much more than he let see the light of day, but whenever I've asked him he's always denied it. 'As soon as I left Oxford', he once said, 'it was like taking the cork out of a bottle.' Not so now. Another evening I remember him, in response to my question, picking up his knife and fork and saying (this was the gist of it, anyway): 'When I wrote poems there were two things crossing on one another—let's call the knife the idea, and the fork the other thing—"inspiration". They crossed on one another and there was the poem. Now I can get one or the other, but not both together.' Obviously I regret not having known him when he was writing more fluently. His MS book of the poems later included in *High Windows* was once exhibited in the university library, and showed 'Forget What Did' and 'High Windows' itself to have been virtually completed on consecutive days. But though the actual production of poems may have slowed almost to a standstill, the personality which created them is still emphatically itself. He is, of course, a distinguished but integral and familiar figure in the university, and being so allows him to escape most of the pressures incumbent on 'writers in residence'. That's to say, he's able to avoid expectations that he should behave exactly like the speakers in his poems, rather than be as he is himself. To a large extent, however, the poems *are* auto-biographical, and even allowing for the personae they adopt, it's easy to see their recurrent themes finding expression in an every-day practical context. Larkin's job, for instance, is in its un-congenial moments the 'sickening poison' we all sometimes feel work to be. But more often it's a welcome discipline and ritual. Much the same is true of social responsibilities. Going out—particularly when you work in a university—often means 'Asking that ass about his fool research'. This doesn't imply, though, that society—for all its disadvantages—isn't also a way of coping with the 'failure and remorse' which accompany solitude.

It's hard to say how deeply Larkin's poems have influenced my own. No doubt very. There's a natural reluctance, however, to act as one's own interpreter in these matters—and in any case the way is barred by his old warning about 'literary understrappers letting you see they know the right people'. But he's certainly helped me more than anyone else to clarify the kind of poetry I want to write, and been marvellous company—often profound, and sometimes extremely funny. I'm back in Oxford now, and I miss him. I saw him shortly before I left. It was lunch time, and I was telling him with a mixture of embarrassment and callow pride that, under the conditions of a mutual acquaintance's will, two letters of mine—both of which had poems in them—had been sold at auction. They'd fetched thirty-two pounds. Scarcely was the figure out of my mouth when Larkin's face lit up. 'Thirty pieces of silver,' he said laughing. 'Plus VAT.'

Instead of a Present

ALAN BENNETT

My first thought was that this whole enterprise is definitely incongruous. A birthday party for Philip Larkin is like treating Simone Weil to a candlelit dinner for two at a restaurant of her choice. Or sending Proust flowers. No. A volume of this sort is simply a sharp nudge in the direction of the grave; and that is a road, God knows, along which he needs no nudging.

And why now in particular? Apparently he is sixty, but when was he anything else? He has made a habit of being sixty; he has made a profession of it. Like Lady Dumbleton he has been sixty for the last twenty-five years. On his own admission there was never a boy Larkin; no young lad Philip, let alone Phil, ever. And I'm not going to supply the textual references: there'll be enough of that going on elsewhere.

Besides, why a *book*? He must be fed up at the sight of books. It's books, books, books every day of his life, and now here's another of the blighters. Why not something more along the lines of a biscuit barrel? Because that's all this collection is, the literary equivalent of an electric toaster (or a Teasmaid perhaps) presented by the divisional manager at an awkward ceremony in the staff canteen, and in the firm's time too. Still, any form of clock would have been a mistake. Better to have played safe and gone for salad servers or even a fish slice. I had an auntie, the manageress of a shoeshop, who every birthday gave me shoe-trees. They were always acceptable.

These are some of the reasons why I feel ill at ease in this doleful jamboree. Added to which there is the question of his name.

Without knowing Mr Larkin, what do I call him? I feel like the student at a dance, suddenly partnered by the Chancellor of the University, who happened to be Princess Margaret. Swinging petrified into the cha-cha he stammered, 'I am not sure what to call you.' The strobe was doused in the Windsor glare: 'Why not try Princess Margaret?' A bleak smile from Hull could be just as disconcerting. *Philip* he plainly is not, though *Larkin* is over-familiar too, suggesting a certain fellow-footing. Being a librarian doesn't help: I've always found them close relatives of the walking dead.

Of course this book is presumably not addressed to the librarian. I imagine all librarians get at sixty is piles. If they're lucky. No, we are addressing the real Larkin, the one who feels shut out when he sees fifteen-year-olds necking at bus-stops. But that's risky too: authors resent the knowledge of themselves they have volunteered to their readers, and one can never address them in the light of it without turning to some extent into a lady in a hat.

Whether as Larkin, Philip Larkin or plain Philip, his name is bound to turn up on every page of this book. Names strike more than they stroke, and I would like to think of him wincing as he reads, staggering under repeated blows from his own name, Larkin buffeted not celebrated. I should be disappointed in him, too, did he not harbour doubts about the whole enterprise, echoing Balfour's remark: 'I am more or less happy when being praised, not very uncomfortable when being abused, but I have moments of uneasiness when being explained.'

It's very gingerly, therefore, that I say my thank you. For what? Often simply because his poems happen to coincide with my own life. And, yes, I know that is what one is supposed to feel, and that is Art. But it's not art that stood me for the two minutes' silence on the parade ground at Coulsdon one November morning in 1952 when the Comet came looming low out of the fog, as in 'Naturally The Foundation Will Bear Your Expenses'. Or put me in a Saturday train from Leeds on a slow and stopping journey southwards, the only empty seats reserved for a honeymoon couple who got on at Doncaster. One of the first of his poems I read was 'I Remember, I Remember', and it was this sense of coincidence, even collocation, that made me go on to read more. It isn't my favourite among his poems, but it's the one that made me realize that someone who admitted his childhood was 'a forgotten boredom' might be talking to me.

I had always had a sneaking feeling my childhood didn't come up to scratch, even at the time; and when I began at the usual age to think there might be some question of becoming 'a writer' (I do not say writing) the want of this apparently essential period seemed crucial. In all the books I had read childhoods were either idyllic or deprived. Mine had been neither. In point of memories I was a non-starter. I had not spent hours in the crook of a great tree devouring Alice or Edgar Rice Burroughs. I read (and even then patchily . . . I never *devoured* anything) *Hotspur*, *Wizard*, *Champion* and *Knock-Out*, not quite the ore of art. It's true that for a long time I too went to bed early, but most children did in those days, with no effect on the percentage turning out to be Proust. I scanned my childhood for eccentrics and found none. I had an aunt who had played the piano in the silent cinema; her music is still in the piano stool today (snap again), but there was nothing odd about her, apart from her large, elderly bust; and there was no shortage of those either.

My school was dull too. It wasn't old. It wasn't new. There was not even a kindly schoolmaster who put books into my hands. I think one may have tried to, but it was not until I was sixteen and a bit late in the day. Another boy had shown me Stephen Spender's *World Within World*, or at any rate the bits dealing with homosexuality, the references to which (while pretty opaque by today's standards) were thought rather daring in 1951. Spender had been befriended by the music master, Mr Greatorex, who had told young Stephen that although he was unhappy now there would come a time when he would begin to be happy and then he would be happier than most. I took great comfort from this, except that I wasn't particularly unhappy (that was the trouble); but the thought that I was about to get the

Greatorex treatment, that a master in my dull day-school had divined beneath my awkwardness the forlorn and troubled essence, produced in me a reaction of such extravagant enthusiasm and wanting to be 'brought out' that the master in question (who had merely suggested I might like to read his *New Statesman* from time to time) scuttled straight back into his shell. It was further proof that literature and life (or my life at any rate) were different things. For the time being, anyway. At Oxford I was sure it would be different.

So to Oxford I duly went, changing stations at Sheffield and probably taking for a train-spotter that balding man at the end of the platform eating a pie. That I had still not acquired a past hit me the minute I entered the lodge of my college. It was piled high with trunks: trunks pasted with ancient labels, trunks that had holidayed in Grand Hotels, travelled first-class on liners, trunks painted with four, nay even *five* initials (that's another sympathetic thing about Larkin, the bare essentials of his name). These shabby, confident trunks had stood in this lodge before. They were the trunks of fathers that were now the trunks of sons, trunks of generations. These trunks spoke memory. I had two shameful Antler suitcases that I had gone with my mother to buy at Schofields in Leeds—an agonizing process, since it had involved her explaining to the shop assistant, a class my mother always assumed were persons of some refinement, that the cases were for going to Oxford with on a scholarship and were these the kind of thing? They weren't. One foot across the threshold of the college lodge and I saw it, and hurried to hide them beneath my cold bed. By the end of the first term I hadn't acquired much education but I got myself a decent, second-hand trunk.

It didn't stop at the trunk either. Class, background, culture, accent . . . all that was going to have to be acquired second-hand too. Had I read 'I Remember, I Remember' in 1955, when *The Less Deceived* came out, I might have been spared the trouble. Though I doubt it. Poems tell you what you know already, and I still had it to learn. Besides I didn't read poetry. I thought I read Auden, but to tell the truth—except in the shortest poems—I

never got beyond the first dozen or so lines without being completely lost. One of the good things about Larkin is that he still
has you firmly by the hand as you cross the finishing line. Whereas
reading Auden is like doing a parachute drop: for a while the
view is wonderful, but then you end up on your back in the
middle of a ploughed field and in the wrong county. I heard
Auden give his inaugural lecture as Professor of Poetry at Oxford
in 1956. That put the tin hat on any lingering thoughts of Literature (one of my problems was that I still thought of both Literature
and Life as having capital letters). Here were, 'blinding theologies
of fruit and flowers', a monogrammed set of myths and memories
carried over from a bulging childhood, and not in Antler suitcases
either. Obsessions, landscapes, favourite books, even (one's heart
sank) the Icelandic sagas. If writing meant passing this sort of kit
inspection, I'd better forget it.

Dissolve to 1966. Life, love and literature were all long since in
the lower case and I had drifted into show business. I was looking
for ideas to beef up a comedy series. It was practically a clause in
the BBC charter at that time that comedy sketches should be
linked only with vocal numbers. I was after something that bit
classier. My producer, Patrick Garland, suggested filming poems,
gave me *The Less Deceived*, and I read 'I Remember, I Remember'.
I think I had realized by then that to write one doesn't need
credentials, but I must be the only one of his readers who came to
Larkin as an alternative to Alma Cogan.

If presents are in order I would like him to have that sound,
part sigh, part affirmation, that I heard once in Zion Chapel,
Settle, in Yorkshire, after I'd read 'MCMXIV'. And another
sound: reading Larkin in public, I've sometimes followed on
with Stevie Smith's 'Not Waving But Drowning' which contains
the line

> Poor chap, he'd always loved larking
> And now he's dead

Of course, being the sort of person he was the poor chap would
have; and half thinking it a pun—and not inappropriate at that—
one or two people in the audience *mew* to themselves.

He would also appreciate something my mother said. My brother had gone to Athens. She was asked where he was but could not remember. 'It begins with an A' she said. 'Oh, I know. Abroad.'

I am abroad writing this in another place beginning with A, America. He would not thank me for New York, I imagine, but if he does not feel at home here he would not feel out of place among streets like Greene and Grand and Great Jones, the cast-iron district which I see from my window. I would give him, too, any work by Edward Hopper, whose paintings could often pass as illustrations to the poems of Larkin; and in particular 'People In The Sun' (1960).

Finally, something I saw scrawled up in the subway. On the wall someone has written 'Pray for me'. Another hand has added 'Sure'.

Larkin's Music

DONALD MITCHELL

> So life was never better than
> In nineteen sixty-three
> (Though just too late for me)—
> Between the end of the *Chatterley* ban
> And the Beatles' first LP.

In his generous inscription on the fly-leaf of *All What Jazz*
Philip wrote: 'To Donald, who's responsible for it all'. I would
not care—or dare—to make any such claim. But I can claim to
have stimulated Philip to the composition of the quatrain which
accompanied the inscription and which hitherto has remained
unpublished (and surely it cannot be the good fortune of every
contributor to add to the canon?):

> When Coote roared: 'Mitchell! what about this jazz?'
> Don thought, That's just the talent Philip has;
> And even if he finds it bad or worse
> At least he'll have less time for writing verse. . . .

An annotation or two of that elegant bit of poetic licence—
because of course I thought nothing of the kind—will reveal the
facts. For a start, the roaring 'Coote' was not some creature of
Philip's imagination, in the spirit of Isherwood's and Upward's
fantasy world, Mortmere, but none other than the late Sir Colin
Coote, the patrician, High Tory Editor of the *Daily Telegraph*
when I was a member—the junior member—of the music staff.

(Coote, it was, who reduced me to silence at my interview by asking me in blandest voice 'how *amused*' was I by the thought of joining the paper, a story Philip has always relished.)

Thus it was through my association with the *Telegraph* (certainly an amusing one in view of my political convictions) that Philip came to be appointed the paper's Jazz correspondent. Someone in the features department, in bold and innovatory mood, thought it was time that the *Telegraph* accorded Jazz official recognition. But whom should we approach, to invite to be our Jazz critic? (The *Telegraph*, you will understand, was not rich in connections in this sphere.) By a lucky chance I was in the office that day, took part in the discussion and proposed Philip. (In any case, no other candidates emerged.) Coote—was *he* amused by the proposal, I wonder? —approved; and the deal was done.

Philip's name flew to my lips that day in Fleet Street, not only because I was aware of his profound knowledge of and sympathy with Jazz, but also because I shared his enthusiasm for it. Indeed, some of my earliest memories of Philip, from the days when he first joined the University of Hull (we met through a mutual friend, Peter Coveney), evoke musical memories too: convivial gatherings around the gramophone at Cottingham. All this was a new and stimulating experience for me. For while I had known, as a young man, one other poet—the wild, eccentric but remarkably endowed E. H. W. Meyerstein—his passions were relatively orthodox: Beethoven, Berlioz, and Mendelssohn, for example. I found it altogether unusual and surprising that Philip's ears were excited by Louis Armstrong, Duke Ellington and Pee Wee Russell.

Mention of Armstrong reminds me that the publication of Philip's writings on Jazz resulted in the creation of more than one new poem: not only the dedicatory quatrain but also the closing paragraph of the long autobiographical Introduction that he wrote to preface the collection. Armstrong is one of the key names to surface in a coda, both comic and elegiac, which is itself a prose poem. It has been widely remarked upon but its quotation here is obligatory, so revealing is it of the power of the feeling that this music released in the Jazz correspondent of the *Daily Telegraph*:

> My readers . . . Sometimes I wonder whether they really exist. . . . Sometimes I imagine them, sullen fleshy inarticulate men, stockbrokers, sellers of goods, living in thirty-year-old detached houses among the golf courses of Outer London, husbands of ageing and bitter wives they first seduced to Artie Shaw's 'Begin the Beguine' or 'the Squadronaires' 'The Nearness of You'; fathers of cold-eyed lascivious daughters on the pill, to whom Ramsay Macdonald is coeval with Rameses II, and cannabis-smoking jeans-and-bearded Stuart-haired sons whose oriental contempt for 'bread' is equalled only by their insatiable demand for it; men in whom a pile of scratched coverless 78s in the attic can awaken memories of vomiting blindly from small Tudor windows to Muggsy Spanier's 'Sister Kate', or winding up a gramophone in a punt to play Armstrong's 'Body and Soul'; men whose first coronary is coming like Christmas; who drift, loaded helplessly with commitments and obligations and necessary observances, into the darkening avenues of age and incapacity, deserted by everything that once made life sweet. These I have tried to remind of the excitement of jazz, and tell where it may still be found.

One might think that the whole enterprise finds the justification in that one bit of superb verbal music; but that would do an injustice to the importance of the Introduction as a whole, which contains in fact a classic statement—*the* classic statement—of Larkin's anti-modernist position, which he argues in images as vivid as those on which he floats his final prose-poem:

> My own theory is that [the genesis of modernism] is related to an imbalance between the two tensions from which art springs: these are the tension between the artist and his material, and between the artist and his audience, and that in the last 75 years or so the second of these has slackened or even perished. . . . Piqued at being neglected, he has painted portraits with both eyes on the same side of the nose, or smothered a model with paint and rolled her over a blank canvas. He has designed a dwelling-house to be built underground. He has written poems

resembling the kind of pictures typists make with their machines during the coffee break, or a novel in gibberish, or a play in which the characters sit in dustbins. He has made a six-hour film of someone asleep. He has carved human figures with large holes in them. And parallel to this activity ('every idiom has its idiot', as an American novelist has written) there has grown up a kind of critical journalism designed to put it over. The terms and the arguments vary with circumstances, but basically the message is: Don't trust your eyes, or ears, or understanding. They'll tell you this is ridiculous, or ugly, or meaningless. Don't believe them. You've got to work at this: after all, you don't expect to understand anything as important as art straight off, do you?... After all, think what asses people have made of themselves in the past by not understand-ing art—you don't want to be like that, do you? And so on, and so forth. Keep the suckers spending.

One may agree or disagree. I am not sure that I do not agree in principle while questioning Larkin's actual demonology (Picasso, Pound, etc.: I would adduce a different list of names). But there can be no questioning of the central importance the statement has to any consideration of his aesthetic as a poet. The negative credo, so to speak, represents the obverse of—but perhaps is also re-sponsible for—all the strengths of Larkin's verse: its precision, clarity, formal mastery and above all its marvellous rhythmic organization.

I seem to have lapsed into a kind of musical vocabulary, so it may not be inappropriate to praise Larkin for his *scoring*: he places his words with the same kind of scrupulous care for pitch and timbre that we find in the anti-modernist Britten or modern-ist (!) Stravinsky. It is surely no accident that we find all these musical qualities in a poem of Larkin's, 'Love Songs in Age', that takes as its topic the very music that means so much to him, music 'each frank submissive chord' of which

> Had ushered in
> Word after sprawling hyphenated word,
> And the unfailing sense of being young

Spread out like a spring-woken tree, wherein
  That hidden freshness sung,
  That certainty of time laid up in store
  As when she played them first. . . .

A lyric, one might think, that in technical organization in some
sense deliberately reflects the model 'lyrics' of the love songs
which are so poignantly resurrected while at the same time transcending them. The extraordinary way in which 'Love Songs' is
virtually through-composed, a continuity which erases the con-
ventional strophic pattern and preserves unbroken the seamless
rhythmic flow, is only one feature which distinguishes the poem
from the lyrics one supposes the protagonist to be recollecting. It
is also a poem that embodies a musical experience that contrasts
somewhat with the bleak tone and black imagery—'vomiting
blindly from small Tudor windows'—of the Introduction. Poignant maybe, but not savagely pessimistic.

Our critic, as the Introduction discloses, is a man of powerful
convictions and it would have been strange indeed if the modernism he denounces in the high arts (Picasso, *et al.*) were not similarly
trounced when it raises its ugly head in Jazz. John Coltrane, for
example, who found no favour while he was alive, and whose
death did nothing at all to diminish Larkin's sense of outrage:

> Virtually the only compliment one can pay Coltrane is one of
> stature. If he was boring, he was enormously boring. If he was
> ugly, he was massively ugly. To squeak and gibber for 16 bars
> is nothing; Coltrane could do it for 16 minutes, stunning the
> listener into a kind of hypnotic state in which he read and
> re-read the sleeve-note and believed, not of course that he was
> enjoying himself, but that he was hearing something significant.
> Perhaps he was. Time will tell. I regret Coltrane's death, as I
> regret the death of any man, but I can't conceal the fact that it
> leaves in jazz a vast, a blessed silence.

Some obituary. Not many of Larkin's denunciations are as
lengthy as that or so lethal. His dispatch of the Beatles is perhaps
more characteristic. 'What about the Beatles?', he asks himself in
1963; and replies:

'With the Beatles' (Parlophone) suggests that their jazz content is nil, but that, like certain sweets, they seem wonderful until you are suddenly sick. Up till then it's nice, though.

One trembles a little to think of the obituary John Lennon's bizarre death might have prompted.

But how different the tone is when sympathetic, when Larkin responds to Larkin's music, music, that is, that 'makes me tap my foot, grunt affirmative exhortations, or even get up and caper round the room'. In particular, his assessments of players who have his admiration are no less than miniature portraits—and more than that, *sound*-portraits, so precisely coloured is the choice of words. Here for instance is Larkin on James 'Bubber' Miley:

> Miley was a growl trumpeter, and a great user of mutes to give his tone emotional colour. There was nothing new in this: it was at least as old as King Oliver. But Miley's was different: his tone had a snarling, gobbling savagery that stabbed through the coltish orchestrations with primitive authenticity.

Perhaps my favourite Larkin portrait is that of the great clarinet player, Pee Wee Russell:

> No one familiar with the characteristic excitement of his solos, their lurid snuffling, asthmatic voicelessness, notes leant on till they split, and sudden passionate intensities, could deny the uniqueness of his contribution to jazz.

'Snarling, gobbling savagery', 'lurid snuffling, asthmatic voice-lessness'. Not only wonderfully accurate descriptions, but as close to the *sound* of those unique styles as words can get. What a music critic Philip could have been, had he had more time for it!

The Anthologist

JOHN GROSS

The title I have chosen is perhaps a little misleading, since a full scholarly consideration of Larkin's labours as an anthologist would have to take into account *New Poems 1958*, which he edited with Louis MacNeice and Bonamy Dobrée (most of the actual work, according to B. C. Bloomfield's ever-helpful bibliography, being carried out by Larkin and Dobrée), and the *Poetry Supplement* which he compiled for the Poetry Book Society in 1974. Still, for the great majority of his readers—and for present purposes—to talk of the anthologist is quite simply to talk of *the* anthology. Or *that* anthology, many would doubtless prefer to say. For although *The Oxford Book of Twentieth-Century English Verse* has gone through several impressions by now, and although it carries some notable commendations on its dustjacket, it can still readily provoke the disappointment or scandalized disbelief which greeted it on its first appearance—in a number of forceful reviews and even more, one found, in conversation among some of the poet's most impassioned admirers. Not everyone may have gone as far as Donald Davie, 'recoiling aghast from page after page', but many were only too willing to endorse Davie's general complaint that the book represents a perverse triumph of philistinism, the cult of the amateur, the wrong kind of post-modernism, the weakest kind of Englishry. To restore Thomas Hardy to his rightful position was one thing, but did it have to entail the reinstatement of J. C. Squire, Francis Brett Young, Susan Miles, Julian Birdbath?

Larkin himself, in his preface, gives a brief account of how he came to make his final selection. Striving to hold a balance between all the different considerations (unspecified) which pressed on him, he found that his material fell into three groups: 'poems representing aspects of the talents of poets judged either by the age or by myself to be worthy of inclusion, poems judged by me to be worthy of inclusion without reference to their authors, and poems judged by me to carry with them something of the century in which they were written'. This is the short answer to Larkin's critics, in its way, but altogether too short. It leaves too many loopholes and begs too many questions; above all it suggests— or would, if we didn't know otherwise—that we are in the presence of the typical anthologist as once described by Randall Jarrell, 'a sort of Gallup Poll with connections'. Whereas we are in the presence of Philip Larkin, and when someone as gifted and independent chooses to work hand in glove with 'the century' or 'the age' he is surely proposing (although he may be too modest to say so himself) a bold and carefully-pondered act of submission. Submission to the idea that beyond individual taste and predilection, and most certainly beyond the edicts of schools, groups, movements and critical law-givers, there exists something called literature in all its swarming multiplicity, something very nearly as various and not to be hemmed in as the life it springs from.

Inevitably such openness has its limits. There are omissions (of poets rather than poems) which it makes all the harder to justify, and it does not prevent some of the inclusions from looking decidedly half-hearted, the most transparent of token gestures. I tend to agree with Donald Davie, in fact, when he detects a vein of positive cynicism in the book. Only it is the cynicism which seems to me inseparable, for a powerful mind, from tolerance, the private grimace while democratic requirements are fulfilled. And a democratic impulse, with whatever reservations, is one of the features which distinguishes Larkin's anthology: not only on account of its eclecticism, but in the feeling for common humanity which marks so much of the work included, a feeling which can be seen at its most heightened in a poem like Chesterton's 'Gold

Leaves', where heroic fantasies subside with the passing years, and in their place

> a great thing in the street
> Seems any human nod . . .

There remains a good deal to argue over. One can applaud an editor's general principles without necessarily going along with their detailed application, and I don't suppose that I am the only reader to have found that this is one anthology where familiarity does not gradually induce a comfortable settled response, that I still see-saw between gratitude for this and irritation at that. What does remain constant, on the other hand, and what only deepens, is one's pleasure in exploring what might be called the actively Larkinesque element in the book. We read Anatole France, as somebody said (in the days when people used to read Anatole France), in order to find out what Anatole France has been reading, and we read a selection of poems chosen by Philip Larkin in order to find out what Philip Larkin has been selecting —and why.

Sometimes, admittedly, this means no more than a mild stirring of biographical curiosity. What led him back to Sagittarius's verses about the outbreak of war, for instance? One wonders whether he read them when they first appeared, whether they are bound up with his own memories of that jittery September week-end. At other times, image calls out to image: the Odeon flashing fire in Betjeman's 'The Metropolitan Railway' ('Cancer has killed him. Heart is killing her') establishes a melancholy kinship with the Odeon which the honeymoon couples can see from the train window in 'The Whitsun Weddings'. And naturally there is much to mull over in considering Larkin's choice from Hardy or Auden or any of his other known favourites and more obvious precursors. The selection of work by Robert Graves, for example, seems to me oddly inadequate, even a bit grudging, but my sense of disappointment fades as soon as I am reminded that one poem which it does include is 'A Slice of Wedding Cake'— the one about the scores of lovely, gifted girls who marry im-

possible men, the one which reads uncannily like a Larkin poem
before its time.

It is far less a question of possible influences on Larkin, however, than of Larkin's influence on the way in which the poems
he has chosen get read. In many cases, no doubt, on whether they
get read at all. But in directing our attention to a poem he is also
putting us on the alert for the qualities in it which appeal to him
in particular. Often they turn out to be qualities which might have
appealed to anyone; sometimes, alas, we draw a blank. But again
and again, or so I find, our feelings become more fully engaged
and our response is sharpened as we register affinities, cross-
currents, reverberations.

A few examples. E. Nesbit on 'the things that matter' ('For-
getting seems such silly waste!'). Laurence Binyon on 'the silence
of the tide/ That buries the playground of children'. Masefield:

> Best trust the happy moments. What they gave
> Makes men less fearful of the certain grave. . . .

Conversely, Gerald Gould warning us that 'the stuff of moments
is too perilous'. (Gould's is one reputation that a reader might
reasonably have assumed to be sunk beyond salvage; but how
moving the extract from his poem 'Monogamy' is, for all its
awkward patches.) Joseph Campbell's Irish antiquary, with his
'odds and ends of ancientry'. The old woman and the child in
Frances Cornford's poem, helplessly old and helplessly young.
Reflections on solitariness: 'I thought how strange we grow when
we're alone. . . .' (Sassoon). On flawed relationships: '. . . all our
lives long/ We are still fated to do wrong' (Graves again). On the
world which 'unattractive, unnoticeable people' somehow make
for themselves (Blunden). Ruth Pitter's fine poem 'But for Lust'
('But for passion we could rest. . . .'). E. J. Scovell's equally fine
'After Midsummer', where even children 'bring our thoughts to
death'—

> Whose force of life speaks of the distant future,
> Their helplessness of helpless animal nature. . . .

The calm landscape and townscape of Edwin Muir's 'Suburban

Dream', its afternoon tranquillity soon to be broken as 'the masters' come tramping home from office and committee-room.

In some of these instances it is nothing more than a cadence, a tone of voice, that puts one in mind of Larkin himself. Elsewhere it can be a setting (as in Andrew Young's 'Last Snow', Davie's 'Industrial Essex', the despised J. C. Squire's far from despicable 'Winter Nightfall'), or a novelistic cameo (John Cowper Powys confronts unprepossessing A. N. Other in a hotel writing room), or a congenial theme: the impermanence of things, the sudden stab of happiness, the woe that is in marriage (this last handled grimly or wanly or sardonically according to temperament). No shortage of poems about illness, either, or about the indignities of old age. And while one would not want to be guilty of anything as primitive, as Balokowskian, as totting up equine analogues to 'At Grass'—still, it is hard not to be struck by the number of poems about horses that Larkin has included; and beyond that, of poems about animals in general, and man's inhumanity to beast in particular (expressed even more starkly by James Stephens in 'The Cage' than by Larkin himself in 'Take One Home for the Kiddies'). A. Alvarez might well contend that there is plenty of evidence here to support his view that the horses in 'At Grass' belong to 'the world of the R.S.P.C.A.'. Nothing wrong with that; but I think that Larkin has a feeling for the creatureliness of creatures which goes deeper than such a phrase would suggest. It is the feeling which lies at the root of one of the most beautiful of his own shorter poems, 'First Sight' ('Lambs that learn to walk in snow . . .'), and which comes out, in varying degrees, in many of the poems to which he has been drawn—supremely, in Lawrence, but also in the glimpse of the imprisoned panther in Stevie Smith's 'Valuable', the comic pigeons in Norman Mac-Caig's 'Wild Oats', the dogs ('You can feel them feeling mastery, doubt, chagrin') in Day-Lewis's 'Sheepdog Trials in Hyde Park'.

Clearly it is the second- and third-division poets who stand to gain most by being anthologized, and the better a poem is, the less likely it is that an anthologist will modify our response. Can it make any conceivable difference if we read, say, Auden's 'This

Lunar Beauty' in Larkin's selection, rather than as reprinted by Yeats in *his* Oxford Book? Just possibly it can, if we bring to our reading memories of Larkinesque irony on the one hand (the domesticated moonlight of 'Sad Steps'), and high Yeatsian romance (the phases of the moon, the full moon in March) on the other. Only a very small difference, however, the slightest of shifts in our angle of vision. To claim more would merely be fanciful. But where an Auden is scarcely affected, the achievement of a lesser figure, a Charlotte Mew or a Wilfrid Gibson, can be brought into bright new focus. With dozens of minor and not-such-very-minor poets, Larkin persuades us to pause where we might have hurried by, to begin doing justice to qualities which we have disregarded: this death-suited visitant has a life-restoring touch.

Robert Lowell said that the Oxford anthology was 'like a poem, a Larkin, not the best, but the longest to write'. If one thinks of some of the book's limitations, such a judgement will seem extravagant; if one thinks of the last fifty or sixty pages, it will seem absurd. (It would surely have made better sense for Larkin to have set his cut-off date ten years or so earlier, rather than attempting a token selection from the work of his juniors.) Yet there is a core of essential truth in Lowell's tribute. Not only do a great many of the choices in the anthology bear the stamp of Larkin's outlook and personality; they also cohere and interreact, so that we are left with a distinctive picture of the world. The result is a book to live with, a book which deserves a permanent place in the Larkin canon.

Nothing To Be Said

GEORGE HARTLEY

My poetry magazine *Listen*, 1954 to 1962, was fortunate enough, like Grigson's *New Verse*, to appear at a time when a new spirit was appearing in English poetry and early enough to promote the work of an emerging major poet.

My literary association and subsequent friendship with this poet, Philip Larkin, dates from 1953, when, shortly after the first issue of *Listen* had gone to press, I found in the local library his first collection of poems *The North Ship* (1945). Although at this date he hadn't achieved a consistent style, he had written some moving and memorable lines, such as these closing cadences on memories: 'Like fallen apples, they will lose/ Their sweetness at the bruise,/ And then decay.'

Larkin responded to my request for new poems promptly, and over the next eight years was a contributor to all but two numbers. Of the first three poems Larkin sent to me, 'Spring' and 'Dry-Point' were recognizably by the same man who had written the lines on memories; but the third, 'Toads', added qualities they lacked—wit, humour, and the dramatization of the speaking voice: a unique tone, an individual style, but also a new insight into a commonplace experience, the desire to escape from the dull routine of work. Work is compared to a toad that squats on his life and he considers whether he can use his wit to 'drive the brute off'. Then follows a comic catalogue of characters who live on their wits: 'Lecturers, lispers,/ Losels, loblolly-men, louts'. The heavy alliteration, the archaic words, give the alternatives to a world of work the unreality of fantasy. In fact the courage to

'Shout *stuff your pension*!' is seen as 'the stuff/ That dreams are made on'. This leads to the admission that there is an inner toad (cowardice) and that it is impossible to lose either toad 'when you have both'. Both the honesty and the humour make this self-depreciation acceptable because they free it from any suggestion of self-pity.

In all three poems I could see a distinctive way of looking at life, distorted perhaps, but openly acknowledging its own distortion: a quality, that for want of a better word, we usually call vision. No amount of technical mastery can compensate a poet for its lack. 'Spring' and 'Dry-Point' also reveal essential themes. 'Spring' ends with the lines 'And those she has least use for see her best,/ Their paths grown craven and circuitous/ Their visions mountain clear, their needs immodest.' Feeling and attitude here are both central in Larkin's poems, and he summarized them clearly in a letter to me, of April 1955, in response to my request for a new title for his first Marvell Press collection: 'I especially didn't want an "ambiguous" title, or one that made any claims to policy or belief: this (*The Less Deceived*) would however give a certain amount of sad-eyed (and clear-eyed) realism, and if they did pick up the context they might grasp my fundamentally passive attitude to poetry (and life too, I suppose) which believes that the agent is always more deceived than the patient, because action comes from desire, and we all know that desire comes from wanting something we haven't got, which may not make us any happier when we have it. On the other hand suffering—well, there is positively no deception about that. No one *imagines* their suffering.' The 'context' is the poem 'Deceptions' (originally 'The Less Deceived') and its allusion to a speech of Ophelia's: 'I was the more deceived'.

This idea that the passive observer (the poet) sees more clearly through the big 'illusions' in life, and perhaps therefore has a greater sensitivity to the reality of pain and suffering, underlies many of Larkin's poems, but sometimes also emerges as explicit statements. In 'Dry-Point' the 'bubble' of illusions of fulfilment is burst to reveal the grey and arid landscape of reality, but the poem ends with a yearning image of an 'Intensely far . . . pad-locked cube of light'. Here is the first expression of the need to transcend the limitations of human experience that appears inter-mittently in Larkin's poetry, the 'High windows' and what lies beyond them: 'the deep blue air, that shows/ Nothing, and is nowhere and is endless'.

The contents of the second issue of *Listen* pleased me as a whole, but Larkin's group of poems was so outstanding that I wrote to him suggesting that I could devote the whole of the next number to his work or, if he preferred, a separate pamphlet. His reply was discouraging: 'Regarding your pamphlet venture, I write so little that is any good that I am not in a position to commit myself at present.'

Later in the year he sent me 'Poetry of Departures'. Once again a universal need 'to get away from it all' is seen as romantic escapism, and is rejected with an amiable irony that makes its negative conclusion (that to chuck up everything would at once create the object of re-creating the same 'reprehensibly perfect' lifestyle) seem curiously positive. Seen from the perspective of flat dull Hull, how consoling that one didn't have to go haring off to Greek islands, like Durrell or Bernard Spencer, to write exciting stuff.

This poem convinced me of the existence of an *œuvre*. Larkin's phrase 'pamphlet venture' suddenly sounded pejorative (his own pamphlet *XX Poems*, which I didn't know about at the time, had recently fallen into a critical vacuum). Accordingly I wrote to him to suggest a hard-bound volume of about forty pages. He replied by return: 'Yes, I am quite interested in publishing the size of collection you suggest, provided it didn't cost me anything and was a good job of book production. The only drawback is that, as you may have noticed already, I am coming to work in Hull (librarian of the university) in March, and since my poems are nothing if not personal I am not at the moment sure how I feel about being published quite so near what will be home. I am sure we will be meeting soon after I arrive, so might we postpone any definite decision till then?' Did he suspect that I was the Vice-

Chancellor's secretary's husband or something of that sort? And what would he think of the headquarters of *Listen,* a decaying Victorian cottage sandwiched between a fish-and-chip shop and an off-licence, not to mention its youthful, penniless proprietor? This anxiety must have been real enough at the time, because I did manage to persuade him to send me his manuscript from Belfast.

Four years later Larkin wrote an unsigned account of the publication of *The Less Deceived* for the back of the sleeve of his *Listen* recording. There is no mention of his first impression of the Marvell Press, but he does show his loyalty in a puff for its owner: 'It is rather nice to have a publisher who publishes your poems because he likes them and not because you are somebody's aunt or may one day write a novel.' However, on the day in 1971 the Marvell Press made its farewell to its first premises in Hessle, Yorkshire, Larkin came down with his Rolleiflex and seemed anxious to secure a shot of its proprietor, with both the fish-and-chip shop and off-licence in view.

Larkin said in a recent *Observer* interview: 'I think it very sensible not to let people know what you're like.' Yet over the years he has given many interviews. In them all he has skilfully parried any questions about his private life. Looking through them all, I am struck by his unusual self-insight and his essential emotional honesty. Equally striking is the consistency of his beliefs, views, interests and attitudes, and how faithfully they are reflected in his poetry. He is continually letting people know what he is like in relation to the basic emotional preoccupations he shares with everyone. To know him is to realize that the public statements and the poems are the product of an integrity that goes beyond art and is lived.

Shortly after the first edition of *The Less Deceived* had gone out of print Larkin gave me a copy of his privately printed *XX Poems.* Poem IX ('Waiting for Breakfast') seemed to me better than all the rejected poems in this pamphlet and worthy of a place in *The Less Deceived.* Apart from this the poem is important not only in showing a transition from the vague symbolism of many of the earlier poems to a style based on the concrete details of actual experience and a conversational idiom, but also because it epitomizes a central theme in his work. My attempts to persuade him to include it in the second edition failed. Later he added it to a reprint of *The North Ship* with a note in the introduction that the poem, 'though not noticeably better than the rest shows the Celtic fever abated and the patient sleeping soundly'. Larkin did give me permission, though, to broadcast it in my selection of his work for the BBC Third Programme. In my introduction to this I pointed out that 'the last stanza is addressed to the Muse, a word Larkin would never allow to enter his poetic landscape. The poem expresses the feeling that perhaps romantic love is inimical to poetic creation.' One might think this is precisely why Larkin devalues it, yet he returns to this theme directly on a number of occasions (although his attitude to it gradually changes) and it is implicit in many poems which hinge on his non-involvement and his belief that 'the agent is always more deceived than the patient'.

In 'Love', Larkin considers love as the difficulty of being selfish enough 'To upset an existence/ Just for your own sake' and the 'unselfish side' as being satisfied with 'Putting someone else first/ So that you come off worst'. Having made this comparison, he comes to the conclusion: 'My life is for me./ As well ignore gravity', but it is only 'the bleeder found/ Selfish this wrong way round' who 'is ever wholly rebuffed'. This assertion of individuality by staying on the outside is still presented as an act of will, and even if there is a certain wry regret in 'wholly rebuffed' there is a feeling of being in a superior position.

This is also the case in 'Reasons for Attendance', where he watches through a window young couples dancing 'Solemnly on the beat of happiness' and finds that what draws him is 'that lifted rough-tongued bell/ (Art, if you like) whose individual sound/ Insists I too am individual . . . Therefore I stay outside'. Not just outside the dance hall, but, as many other poems make clear, outside all the main emotional entanglements of most people's lives—love, marriage, children. As Larkin says (making concrete Yeats's phrase 'in dreams begin responsibilities') in the uncollected poem 'Breadfruit': 'Such uncorrected visions end in church/ Or registrar:/ A mortgaged semi—with a silver birch;/ Nippers; the widowed mum; having to scheme/ With money: illness; age'. What's wrong here is that though we may accept the comic view of what can happen to those with 'uncorrected visions', it is absurd to suppose that those with the 'corrected' (and correct) vision are any less likely to have to scheme with illness or age. These last two items are not in the same category as 'nippers' or the 'widowed mum'. Of course, it is one good reason why Larkin rejected the poem. We are only likely to make this kind of objection if the speaker seems to be entirely serious, what some American critics have called the 'reliable speaker' (i.e. someone you would agree with yourself).

'Places, Loved Ones' leads to the recognition that, having missed 'that special one' or 'my proper ground', you are 'Bound, nonetheless, to act/ As if what you settled for/ Mashed you, in fact'; that is, persuade yourself that the second best is what really attracted you. ('Mashed', Edwardian slang, has a punning association.) Yet the poem is also saying that to find the ideal '. . . seems to prove/ You want no choice in where/ To build or whom to love'. Passive non-choosing must lead to 'what you settled for' though, typical of Larkin's subtle distinctions, it is seen as a kind of freedom. A similar sophistry is arrived at in 'No Road'; there, not to prevent 'a world where no such road will run from you to me' becomes 'My will's fulfilment' but willing it would be 'my ailment'. A seeming paradox: passive acceptance as an expression of will, active willing as an illness. Later in Larkin's poems 'What we have settled for' becomes 'What something hidden from us chose'.

The theme of a life sacrificed, as an act of free choice, to truth (or art) is more baldly stated in an uncollected poem, 'Success Story', which starts off with dictionary definitions of 'To fail', traced from the Latin *to deceive* and goes on to deny any such intention: 'Yes. But it wasn't that I played unfair:/ Under fourteen, I sent in six words/ My Chief Ambition to the Editor' . . . *'fat forbidding fruit, go by the board/ Until'*. Easy for the reader to

With Sir John Betjeman on the Humber Ferry during the making of a BBC
Monitor film, 1964

With Anthony Thwaite at the University of East Anglia, 1972

Left to right: Richard Murphy, Douglas Dunn, Philip Larkin and Ted Hughes
at Lockington, East Yorkshire, 1970

With the staff of the Brynmor Jones Library, University of Hull, moving into
the new building, July 1969

supply the six words (I want to be a poet) and the biblical pun nicely suggests the simultaneous attraction and repulsion of sex. With the next stanza comes the acknowledgement 'But that *until* has never come/ And I am starving where I always did'. The 'daylight' (rationalistic) explanation is 'To be ambitious is to fall in love/ With a particular life you haven't got/ And (since love picks your opposite) won't succeed'. But 'late at night' (time of dreams) a 'counter-whispering' claims success. The 'dirty feeding' has been dodged 'at hardly any price—achieve/ Just some pretence about the other thing'. The 'other thing' is poetic success and the pretence that it is of value and worth 'dodging the dirty feeding' for. However, this situation arises out of an exercise of choice.

The more typical Larkin attitude of not choosing as a kind of negative choice reappears in 'The Life with a Hole in it', where the speaker answers the complaint '. . . *you've always done what you want,*' with 'What the old ratbags mean/ Is I've never done what I don't'. Then he compares the life style of the 'shit in the shuttered château', who fits in his writing 'Between bathing and booze and birds', with that of the 'spectacled schoolteaching sod/ (Six kids, and the wife in pod)'. Both are as 'far off as ever' but, later, life is seen as an unequal struggle between 'your wants' and the 'unbeatable slow machine/ That brings you what you'll get'. The comically concealed envy for the hedonistic freedom of the 'shit', the savage satisfaction at escaping the fate of the 'schoolteaching sod', give way to the realization that they, like the speaker, are united by the common fate.

The fact that Larkin doesn't escape this theme is partly because his feelings about it are mixed and always changing; but also, perhaps, it is due to technical dissatisfaction with its expression. Larkin has shown his approval for 'Send No Money', and certainly its combination of ferocity and humour makes it a striking success. Once more the passive life devoted to the pursuit of truth is seen as just another kind of illusion, no better than the one that love, marriage and children bring fulfilment. Larkin's persona, a youth, appeals to an avuncular personification of Time to '*Tell me the truth . . . Teach me the way things go*'. All the other lads are eager to have a go at life, but he thinks 'wanting unfair: It and finding out clash'. Time, seeing 'no green' in his eyes (this reminds us of Larkin's earlier insight 'That how we live measures our own nature'), advises him to *'watch the hail/ Of occurrence clobber life out/ To a shape no one sees'*. Having taken Time's advice, half a lifetime later he sees his face as a 'bestial visor, bent in/ By the blows of what happened to happen'. The final statement, 'What does it prove? Sod all/ In this way I spent youth/ Tracing the trite untransferable/ Truss-advertisement truth', not only dismisses the value of insight into life as coming too late to be applied, but also shows that value to be illusory anyway. 'Truss-advertisement Truth' brilliantly suggests both artificial support and the false promise of continued spiritual potency. The untransferable truth comes into 'Continuing to Live', where regretting that life is not like a game of poker, so that you can discard bad cards, but in fact is more like chess, when 'what you command is clear as a lading-list' leads to the dismal truth 'that, in time,/ We half identify the blind impress/ All our behavings bear'. But there is no satisfaction in this knowledge, 'Since it applied only to one man once,/ And that one dying'.

Clive James found two poems in *High Windows*, 'Sympathy in White Major' and the middle section of 'Livings', cases of 'over-refinement leading to obscurity'. I find neither poem obscure. It is simply that Larkin is inexplicit and suggestive with themes that elsewhere he has dealt with more directly. The speaker in 'Sympathy in White Major' starts by mixing a large gin and tonic to drink 'a private pledge' to a man who *'devoted his life to others'*. It soon becomes clear he is drinking an ironic toast to himself: 'While other people wore like clothes/ The human beings in their days/ I set myself to bring to those/ Who thought I could the lost displays'. These 'other people' are the ones who selfishly 'use' 'human beings' in love and marriage, discarding them like clothes when they are worn out or out of fashion. The speaker has made the choice of the solitary life devoted to preserving the high points in life of those more actively involved in it.

This passive creator links himself to a passive audience: 'It didn't work for them or me', but both share the illusion of being nearer to 'all the fuss' than if they 'missed it separately'. The last stanza is a series of tautological phrases, all dated eulogisms: 'A brick, a trump, a proper sport', and ends 'Here's to the whitest man I know—/ Though white is not my favourite colour'. 'The whitest man', a phrase from the days of the British Raj, guyed in Edwardian Music Hall, is turned into an ambiguity in the last line. Whiteness, or moral worthiness, is also the whiteness of the man untainted by experience, but finally it denotes cowardice: the white feather sent to the Major who wouldn't volunteer for active service, the musical-military pun in the title. Despite the use of a sardonic persona, other poems by Larkin make it clear that he does see his own refusal to join the 'front line' of life as arising from natural timidity, and not just prior involvement in essential services at home.

As a complete contrast to all the 'negative' versions of this theme, the middle section of 'Livings' positively exults in the solitary vocation. The unnamed speaker is a lighthouse keeper; and even though he inhabits a metaphorical lighthouse the diction is vivid and specific: 'Rocks writhe back to sight./ Mussels, limpets,/ Husband their tenacity/ In the freezing slither—/ Creatures, I cherish you!' The narrators of the flanking sections of the triptych (one a don at the time of the Restoration, the other an agricultural salesman in the twenties) do, in however limited a way, share their lives with others; but they have no sense of vocation. The lighthouse keeper, unlike them, is like a priest without acolytes, perpetually celebrating a sacrament: 'Guarded by brilliance/ I set plate and spoon,/ And after, divining-cards,/ Lit shelved liners/ Grope like mad worlds westward'. 'Brilliance' is literally the lighthouse beam; symbolically it is the inner light of the creator. Life goes by, like a ship of fools towards death.

The poem triumphantly vindicates the romantic symbolism of *The North Ship* but without falling into vagueness. It may be that 'Livings' is Larkin's farewell not only to this theme but to all its close relatives. Certainly another piece from *High Windows*,

'Forget What Did', suggests it is: 'Stopping the diary/ Was a stun to memory . . . I wanted them over/ Hurried to burial. . . . And the empty pages?/ Should they ever be filled/ Let it be with observed/ Celestial recurrences,/ The day the flowers come,/ And when the birds go'. Indeed, two pages of the book are filled with cameos of 'celestial recurrences'.

All questions of choice, missed alternatives, opportunities lost, of whether single-minded dedication to art brings its own fulfil-ment, give way in the later poems to the expression that we are all prey to unconscious forces, externally pushed about by crass causality: 'What something hidden from us chose' or 'Whatever happened to happen'. Nevertheless the really menacing external force in the poetry, right from the beginning, is Time itself. This is the well-spring of all the melancholy, for it proves in the end that active participation or passive attention lead to the same inescapable conclusion that 'Whether or not we use it, it goes'. Strong feelings about all time's 'eroding agents' pervade his poetry, and make an early and stark appearance in poem XXVI in *The North Ship*: 'This is the first thing/ I have understood:/ Time is the echo of an axe/ Within a wood'. The echo reverberates throughout his work.

Earlier expressions of a death wish have receded and are being replaced by a real fear of death. Larkin's most recently published poem, 'Aubade', expresses this fear in direct unqualified state-ment:

> This is a special way of being afraid
> No trick dispels. Religion used to try,
> That vast moth-eaten musical brocade
> Created to pretend we never die,
> And specious stuff that says *No rational being*
> *Can fear a thing it will not feel*, not seeing
> That this is what we fear—no sight, no sound,
> No touch or taste or smell, nothing to think with,
> Nothing to love or link with,
> The anaesthetic from which none come round.

That last line recalls 'The Building', the hospital as a secular substitute for cathedrals, where despite votive offerings of flowers the only sacrifice it accepts is life itself.

To complain of this as a distortion of reality would be to ignore the fact that all the poems are principally designed to convey feelings, not ideas. We can take pleasure in their superb craftsmanship as we would with other beautifully wrought objects. For Larkin, the fact that 'time's eroding agents' bring final oblivion, tend to make ambitions and alternative life-styles all equally meaningless, doesn't prevent him from struggling towards some kind of poetic meaning. Many readers who don't have the consolation of a belief in an after-life may try to ignore all reminders of the blankness of death. Such people are not likely to approve of much of Larkin's poetry. 'Nothing To Be Said' sums it all up:

> Hours giving evidence
> Or birth, advance
> On death equally slowly.
> And saying so to some
> Means nothing; others it leaves
> Nothing to be said.

On His Wit

CLIVE JAMES

There is no phrase in Philip Larkin's poetry which has not been turned, but then any poet tries to avoid flat writing, even at the cost of producing overwrought banality. Larkin's dedication to compressed resonance is best studied, in the first instance, through his prose. The prefaces to the re-issues of *Jill* and *The North Ship* are full of sentences that make you smile at their neat richness even when they are not meant to be jokes, and that when they are meant to be jokes—as in the evocation of the young Kingsley Amis at Oxford in the preface to *Jill*—make you wish that the article went on as long as the book. But there is a whole book which does just that: *All What Jazz*, the collection of Larkin's *Daily Telegraph* jazz record review columns which was published in 1970. Having brought the book out, Faber seemed nervous about what to do with it next. I bought two copies marked down to 75p each in a Cardiff newsagents and wish now that I had bought ten. I thought at the time that *All What Jazz* was the best available expression by the author himself of what he believed art to be. Nowadays I still think so, and would contend in addition that no wittier book of criticism has ever been written.

To be witty does not necessarily mean to crack wise. In fact it usually means the opposite: wits rarely tell jokes. Larkin's prose flatters the reader by giving him as much as he can take in at one time. The delight caused has to do with collusion. Writer and reader are in cahoots. Larkin has the knack of donning cap and bells while still keeping his dignity. For years he feigned desperation before the task of conveying the real desperation induced in him by the saxophone playing of John Coltrane. The metaphors can be pursued through the book—they constitute by themselves a kind of extended solo, of which the summary sentence in the book's introductory essay should be regarded as the coda: 'With John Coltrane metallic and passionless nullity gave way to exercises in gigantic absurdity, great boring excursions on not-especially-attractive themes during which all possible changes were rung, extended investigations of oriental tedium, long-winded and portentous demonstrations of religiosity.' This final grandiose flourish was uttered in 1968.

But the opening note was blown in 1961, when Larkin, while yet prepared (cravenly, by his own later insistence) to praise Coltrane as a hard-thinking experimenter, referred to 'the vinegary drizzle of his tone'. In 1962 he was still in two minds, but you could already guess which mind was winning. 'Coltrane's records are, paradoxically, nearly always both interesting and boring, and I find myself listening to them in preference to many a less adventurous set.' Notable at this stage is that he did not risk a metaphor, in which the truth would have more saliently protruded. In May 1963 there is only one mind left talking. To the eighth track of a Thelonius Monk album, 'John Coltrane contributes a solo of characteristic dreariness.'

By December of that same year Larkin's line on this topic has not only lost all its qualifications but acquired metaphorical force. Coltrane is referred to as 'the master of the thinly disagreeable' who 'sounds as if he is playing for an audience of cobras'. This squares up well with the critic's known disgust that the joyous voicing of the old jazz should have so completely given way to 'the cobra-coaxing cacophonies of Calcutta'. In 1965 Larkin was gratified to discover that his opinion of Coltrane's achievement was shared by the great blues-shouter Jimmy Rushing. 'I don't think he can play his instrument,' said Rushing. 'This,' Larkin observed, 'accords very well with my own opinion that Coltrane sounds like nothing so much as a club bore who has been metamorphosed by a fellow-member of magical powers into a pair of bagpipes.' (Note Larkin's comic timing, incidentally: a less witty writer would have put 'metamorphosed into a pair of bagpipes by a fellow-member of magical powers', and so halved the effect.) Later in the same piece he expanded the attack into one of those generally pertinent critical disquisitions in which *All What Jazz* is so wealthy:

> His solos seem to me to bear the same relation to proper jazz solos as those drawings of running dogs, showing their legs in all positions so that they appear to have about fifty of them, have to real drawings. Once, they are amusing and even instructive. But the whole point of drawing is to choose the right line, not drawing fifty alternatives. Again, Coltrane's choice and treatment of themes is hypnotic, repetitive, monotonous: he will rock backwards and forwards between two chords for five minutes, or pull a tune to pieces like someone subtracting petals from a flower.

Later in the piece there is an atavistic gesture towards giving the Devil his due, but by the vividness of his chosen figures of speech the critic has already shown what he really thinks.

'I can thoroughly endorse', wrote Larkin in July 1966, 'the sleeve of John Coltrane's "Ascension" (HMV), which says "This record cannot be loved or understood in one sitting."' In November of the same year he greeted Coltrane's religious suite 'Meditations' as 'the most astounding piece of ugliness I have ever heard'. After Coltrane's death in 1977 Larkin summed up the departed hero's career:

> ... I do not remember ever suggesting that his music was anything but a pain between the ears. ... Was I wrong?

In fact, as we have seen, Larkin had once allowed himself to suggest that the noises Coltrane made might at least be interesting, but by now tentativeness had long given way to a kind of fury, as of someone defending a principle against his own past weakness:

> That reedy, catarrhal tone ... that insolent egotism, leading to 45-minute versions of 'My Favourite Things' until, at any rate in Britain, the audience walked out, no doubt wondering why they had ever walked in ... pretension as a way of life ...

wilful and hideous distortion of tone that offered squeals, squeaks, Bronx cheers and throttled slate-pencil noises for serious consideration . . . dervish-like heights of hysteria.

It should be remembered, if this sounds like a grave being danced on, that Larkin's was virtually the sole dissenting critical voice. Coltrane died in triumph and Larkin had every right to think at the time that to express any doubts about the stature of the deceased genius was to whistle against the wind.

The whole of *All What Jazz* is a losing battle. Larkin was arguing in support of entertainment at a time when entertainment was steadily yielding ground to portentous significance. His raillery against the saxophonist was merely the most strident expression of a general argument which he went on elaborating as its truth became more clear to himself. In a quieter way he became progressively disillusioned with Miles Davis. In January 1962 it was allowed that in an informal atmosphere Davis could produce music 'very far from the egg-walking hushedness' he was given to in the studio. In October of the same year Larkin gave him points for bonhomie:

> According to the sleeve, Davis actually smiled twice at the audience during the evening and there is indeed a warmth about the entire proceedings that makes this a most enjoyable LP.

But by the time of 'Seven Steps to Heaven' a year later, Davis had either lost what little attraction he had or else Larkin has acquired the courage of his convictions:

> . . . his lifeless muted tone, at once hollow and unresonant, creeps along only just in tempo, the ends of the notes hanging down like Dali watches . . .

In 1964 Larkin begged to dissent from the enthusiastic applause recorded on the live album 'Miles Davis in Europe':

> . . . the fact that he can spend seven or eight minutes playing 'Autumn Leaves' without my recognizing or liking the tune confirms my view of him as a master of rebarbative boredom.

A year later he was reaching for the metaphors:

> I freely confess that there have been times recently when
> almost anything—the shape of a patch on the ceiling, a recipe
> for rhubarb jam read upside down in the paper—has seemed
> to me more interesting than the passionless creep of a Miles
> Davis trumpet solo.

But in this case the opening blast was followed by a climb-down:

> Davis is his usual bleak self, his notes wilting at the edges as if
> with frost, spiky at up-tempos, and while he is still not my
> ideal of comfortable listening his talent is clearly undiminished.

This has the cracked chime of a compromise. The notes, though
wilting as if with frost instead of like Dali watches, are nevertheless still wilting, and it is clear from the whole drift of Larkin's
criticism that he places no value on uncomfortable listening as
such. A 1966 review sounds more straightforward:

> . . . for me it was an experience in pure duration. Some of it
> must have been quite hard to do.

But in Larkin's prose the invective which implies values is
always matched by the encomium which states them plainly. He
jokes less when praising than when attacking but the attention
he pays to evocation is even more concentrated. The poem 'For
Sidney Bechet' ('On me your voice falls as they say love should,/
Like an enormous yes,') can be matched for unforced reverence
in the critical prose:

> . . . the marvellous 'Blue Horizon', six choruses of slow blues
> in which Bechet climbs without interruption or hurry from
> lower to upper register, his clarinet tone at first thick and
> throbbing, then soaring like Melba in an extraordinary blend of
> lyricism and power that constituted the unique Bechet voice,
> commanding attention the instant it sounded.

He is similarly eloquent about the 'fire and shimmer' of Bix
Beiderbecke, and of the similes he attaches to Pee Wee Russell
there is no end—Russell's clarinet seems to function in Larkin's
imagination as a kind of magic flute.

The emphasis, in Larkin's admiration for all these artists, is on the simplicity at the heart of their creative endeavour. What they do would not have its infinite implications if it did not spring from elementary emotion. It can be argued that Larkin is needlessly dismissive of Duke Ellington and Charlie Parker. There is plenty of evidence to warrant including him in the school of thought known among modern jazz buffs as 'mouldy fig'. But there is nothing retrograde about the aesthetic underlying his irascibility.

The same aesthetic underlies his literary criticism and everything else he writes. Especially it underlies his poetry. Indeed it is not even an aesthetic: it is a world view, of the kind which invariably forms the basis of any great artistic personality. Modernism, according to Larkin, 'helps us neither to enjoy nor endure'. He defines modernism as intellectualized art. Against intellectualism he proposes not anti-intellectualism—which would be just another coldly willed programme—but trust in the validity of emotion. What the true artist says from instinct, the true critic will hear by the same instinct. There may be more than instinct involved, but nothing real will be involved without it:

> The danger, therefore, of assuming that everything played today in jazz has a seed of solid worth stems from the fact that so much of it is tentative, experimental, private. . . . And for this reason one has to fall back on the old dictum that a critic is only as good as his ear. His ear will tell him instantly whether a piece of music is vital, musical, exciting, or cerebral, mock-academic, dead, long before he can read Don De Michael on the subject, or learn that it is written in inverted nineteenths, or in the Stygian mode, or recorded at the NAACP Festival at Little Rock. He must hold on to the principle that the only reason for praising a work is that it pleases, and the way to develop his critical sense is to be more acutely aware of whether he is being pleased or not.

What Larkin might have said on his own behalf is that critical prose can be subjected to the same test. His own criticism appeals so directly to the ear that he puts himself in danger of being thought trivial, especially by the mock-academic. Like Amis's, Larkin's readability seems so effortless that it tends to be thought of as something separate from his intelligence. But readability *is* intelligence. The vividness of Larkin's critical style is not just a token of his seriousness but the embodiment of it. His wit is there not only in the cutting jokes but in the steady work of registering his interest. It is easy to see that he is being witty when he says that Miles Davis and Ornette Colman stand in evolutionary relationship to each other 'like green apples and stomach-ache'. But he is being equally witty when he mentions Ruby Braff's 'peach-fed' cornet. A critic's language is not incidental to him: its intensity is a sure measure of his engagement and a persuasive hint at the importance of what he is engaged with.

A critical engagement with music is one of the several happy coincidences which unite Larkin's career with Montale's. If Larkin's *Listen* articles on poetry were to be reprinted, the field of comparison would be even more instructive, since there are good reasons for thinking that these two poets come up with remarkably similar conclusions when thinking about the art they practise. On music they often sound like the same man talking. Montale began his artistic career as a trained opera singer and his main area of musical criticism has always been classical music, but he writes about it in the same way Larkin writes about jazz, with unfaltering intelligibility, a complete trust in his own ear, and a deep suspicion of any work which draws inspiration from its own technique. In Italy his collected music criticism is an eagerly awaited book, but then in Italy nobody is surprised that a great poet should have written a critical column for so many years of his life. Every educated Italian knows that Montale's music notices are all of a piece with the marvellous body of literary criticism collected in *Auto da fé* and *Sulla poesia*, and that his whole critical corpus is the natural complement to his poetry. In Britain the same connection is harder to make, even though Larkin has deservedly attained a comparable position as a national poet. In Britain the simultaneous pursuit of poetry and regular critical journalism is regarded as versatility at best. The essential unity of Larkin's various activities is not much remarked.

But if we do not remark it, we miss half of his secret. While maintaining an exalted idea of the art he practises, Larkin never thinks of it as an activity inherently separate from the affairs of everyday. He has no special poetic voice. What he brings out is the poetry that is already in the world. He has cherished the purity of his own first responses. Like all great artists he has never lost touch with the child in his own nature. The language of even the most intricately wrought Larkin poem is already present in recognizable embryo when he describes the first jazz musicians ever to capture his devotion:

> It was the drummer I concentrated on, sitting as he did on a raised platform behind a battery of cowbells, temple blocks, cymbals, tomtoms and (usually) a Chinese gong, his drums picked out in flashing crimson or ultramarine brilliants.

There are good grounds for calling Larkin a pessimist, but it should never be forgotten that the most depressing details in the poetry are seen with the same eye that loved those drums. The proof is in the unstinting vitality of the language.

As in the criticism, so in the poetry wit can be divided usefully into two kinds, humorous and plain. There is not much need to rehearse the first kind. Most of us have scores of Larkin's lines, hemistiches and phrases in our heads, to make us smile whenever we think of them, which is as often as the day changes. I can remember the day in 1962 when I first opened *The Less Deceived* and was snared by a line in the first poem, 'Lines on a Young Lady's Photograph Album': 'Not quite your class, I'd say, dear, on the whole.' What a perfectly timed pentameter! How subtly and yet how unmistakeably it defined the jealousy of the speaker! Who on earth was Philip Larkin? Dozens of subsequent lines in the same volume made it clearer: he was a supreme master of language levels, snapping into and out of a tone of voice as fast as it could be done without losing the reader. Bringing the reader in on it—the deep secret of popular seriousness. Larkin brought the reader in on it even at the level of prosodic technique:

> Flagged, and the figurehead with golden tits
> Arching our way, it never anchors; it's . . .

He got you smiling at a rhyme. 'Church Going' had the 'ruin-bibber, randy for antique'. 'Toads' had the pun on Shakespeare, *Stuff your pension!* being the stuff dreams are made on. You couldn't get half way through the book without questioning, and in many cases revising, your long-nursed notions about poetic language. Here was a disciplined yet unlimited variety of tone, a scrupulosity that could contain anything, an all-inclusive decorum.

In *The Whitsun Weddings*, 'Mr Bleaney' has the Bodies, and 'Naturally The Foundation Will Bear Your Expenses' has the ineffable Mr Lal. 'Sunny Prestatyn' features Titch Thomas, and in 'Wild Oats' a girl painfully reminiscent of Margaret in *Lucky Jim* is finally shaken loose 'after about five rehearsals'. In 'Essential Beauty' 'the trite untransferable/ Truss-advertisement, truth' takes you back to the cobra-coaxing cacophonies of Calcutta, not to mention forward to Amis's nitwit not fit to shift shit. Even *High Windows*, the bleakest of Larkin's slim volumes, has things to make you laugh aloud. In 'The Card-Players' Jan van Hog-speuw and Old Prijck perhaps verge on the coarse, but Jake Balokowsky in 'Posterity' has already entered the gallery of timeless academic portraits, along with Professor Welch and the History Man. '*Vers de Société*' has 'the bitch/ Who's read nothing but *Which*'. In Larkin's three major volumes of poetry the jokes on their own would be enough to tell you that wit is alive and working.

But it is working far more pervasively than that. Larkin's poetry is *all* witty—which is to say that there is none of his language which does not confidently rely on the intelligent reader's capacity to apprehend its play of tone. On top of the scores of fragments that make us laugh, there are the hundreds which we constantly recall with a welcome sense of communion, as if our own best thoughts had been given their most concise possible expression. If Auden was right about the test of successful writing being how often the reader thinks of it, Larkin passed long ago. To quote even the best examples would be to fill half this book, but perhaps it will bear saying again, this time in the context of his poetry, that between Larkin's humorous wit and his plain wit there is no discontinuity. Only the man who invented the golden tits could evoke the black-sailed unfamiliar. To be able to make fun of the randy ruin-bibber is the necessary qualification for writing the magnificent last stanza of 'Church Going'. You need to have been playfully alliterative with the trite untransferable truss-advertisement before you can be lyrically alliterative with the supine stationary voyage of the dead lovers in 'An Arundel Tomb'. There is a level of seriousness which only those capable of humour can reach.

Similarly there is a level of maturity which only those capable of childishness can reach. The lucent comb of 'The Building' can be seen by us only because it has been so intensely seen by Larkin, and it has been so intensely seen by him only because his eyes, behind those thick glasses, retain the naïve curiosity which alone makes the adult gaze truly penetrating. Larkin's poetry draws a bitterly sad picture of modern life but it is full of saving graces, and they are invariably as disarmingly recorded as in a child's diary. The paddling at the seaside, the steamer stuck in the afternoon, the ponies at 'Show Saturday'—they are all done with crayons and coloured pencils. He did not put away childish things and it made him more of a man. It did the same for Montale: those who have ever read about the amulet in *Dora Markus* or the children with tin swords in *Caffè a Rapallo* are unlikely to forget them when they read Larkin.

A third name could be added: Mandelstam. When Mandelstam forecast his own death he willed that his spirit should be resurrected in the form of children's games. All three poets represent, for their respective countrymen, the distilled lyricism of common speech. With all three poets the formal element is highly developed—in the cases of Larkin and Mandelstam to the uppermost limit possible—and yet none of them fails to reassure readers, even during the most intricately extended flight of verbal music, that the tongue in which he speaks is the essential material of his rhythmic and melodic resource.

In Philip Larkin's non-poetic language, the language of extremely well-written prose, despair is expressed through beauty and becomes beautiful too. His argument is with himself and he is bound to lose. He can call up death more powerfully than almost any other poet ever has, but he does so in the commanding voice of life. His linguistic exuberance is the heart of him. Joseph Brodsky, writing about Mandelstam, called lyricism the ethics of language. Larkin's wit is the ethics of his poetry. It brings his distress under our control. It makes his personal unhappiness our universal exultation. Armed with his wit, he faces the worst on our behalf, and brings it to order. A romantic sensibility classically disciplined, he is, in the only sense of the word likely to last, modern after all. By rebuilding the ruined bridge between poetry and the general reading public he has given his art a future, and you can't get more modern than that.

Novels into Poems

ALAN BROWNJOHN

Philip Larkin's two novels came, as did the poems in *The North Ship*, in what he recently described as an upsurge of 'creative relief' after he left Oxford in 1943; and the three books were published in consecutive years (1945, 1946, 1947) when he was still in his early twenties. After this followed a long and disheartening period of transition. These were the years when he was trying to publish a second collection of poems ('with the ponderous title of *In the Grip of Light*') and simultaneously struggling with a third novel. No one would take up the verse: the next collection had to be the set of *XX Poems* privately printed and circulated in 1951. And after five years of effort the novel was abandoned. In the early 1950s he might have felt that he had written himself into failure.

He has always been firmly modest about the two novels, albeit giving different sorts of reason. The reissued *Jill* (1964) appeared with an exuberantly funny introduction, not so much about the book as about his undergraduate friends in wartime Oxford—ending with the brief, self-deprecating hope that *Jill* might receive 'the indulgence traditionally extended to juvenilia'. In an interview published much later, in April 1980, he is equally diffident concerning *A Girl in Winter* (reissued in 1957), but that book was to be seen in quite a different light:

> ... that's a much more sophisticated book, written, shaped, a Virginia Woolf–Henry Green kind of novel. I took much trouble over it but I don't think either [of the two novels] ... is any good ... I don't think my books were novels, they were more kinds of prose poem.

It is possible to discount this modesty, and to enjoy and admire both books (and both *are* good), while still conceding something of the spirit of Larkin's disclaimers. For all their initial lack of reception, the poems written soon after *The North Ship* are moving confidently in the right direction—which is towards *The Less Deceived*, where we find thirteen of the *XX Poems*. But something rather unsuitable was happening in Larkin's prose fiction at the same time, almost as early as the beginning of the second novel.

His own terms may help to suggest the trouble: 'sophisticated', 'written', 'shaped'. The strengths of *Jill* lie partly in its very spontaneity *as* a first novel, the kind of book which uses very vigorously that limited stock of purely personal experiences and feelings on which a young writer is the sole, undisputed authority. The virtues of *A Girl in Winter* are indeed virtues of careful shaping and sensitive calculation; but this was a process which seemed to be luring Larkin away from the experienced realities of the first book towards something more rarefied; and towards an altogether stiffer and more artificial mode of fiction. How hard it actually is to see a 'prose poem' in *Jill*, except in small individual patches. But *A Girl in Winter* aspires from the outset to be something of a 'poetic novel' (not a fashion frowned on in the Neo-Romantic 1940s), and succeeds in that dangerous enterprise much less convincingly than *Jill* succeeds in more straightforward ambitions.

'Wedding Wind' is therefore a strangely helpful poem, displaying a fascinating convergence of Larkin's aspirations in prose and poetry at the time. It offers a brief, cryptic narrative reminiscent of the novels in mood and atmosphere, and a cluster of images almost all derived from or related to passages in them: the wind and the wedding night themselves, candlelight, a thread of beads, the reviving power of water, even the woman setting down a chipped pail and staring (she crops up almost verbatim in *A Girl in Winter*, on p. 120 in the 1964 edition). 'Wedding Wind' (it dates from 1946) is a beautiful, mysteriously resonant narrative excursion of a kind he did not continue to write. And when, somewhere and somehow in the late 1940s, the humour and sheer particularity, the power of speaking directly from personal experience, all so apparent in the first novel, begin to enter into poems made with the skill and delicacy of the second, Larkin has reached the stage of his mature poetry and has finished with fiction.

The plot of *Jill* is simple, and unfolds with nothing more unexpected than one extended, very convenient flashback. On the first page we join the working-class scholarship boy, John Kemp (who bears absolutely no resemblance to the author), as he arrives by train in Oxford in the second autumn of the war. At the very moment John shyly opens the door of his shared college rooms (and shows what he is, unmistakably, by dress and demeanour) the principal theme of the novel is announced: his hearty room-mate, Christopher, is already throwing a tea-party with John's crockery, and the social gulf yawns very wide. Ten years before John Braine's *Room at the Top*, with its hero who indulges a detailed, knowledgeable envy of the fabric of middle-class living, in *Jill* Larkin pins down, page by page, the same experience of the minutiae of class difference as exposed in ordinary social intercourse. John Kemp's college scout knows instinctively that John is a scholar, not a gentleman commoner; John watches with awe and incomprehension the way in which Christopher exhales cigarette smoke 'like cloudy breath' (he tries, and cannot do this himself); he goggles at the audacity of Christopher's mother biting 'hugely' into her teacake without cutting it; he is among people who will use the word 'bastard' in front of a *girl*! Altogether, John's own grubby diligence and application in plodding through life falls desperately short of the admired confidence of these 'fierce and careless' beings.

His admiration is not banished, or even checked, when he overhears Christopher and his affected girl friend Elizabeth talking about him:

> . . . he heard Elizabeth say:
>   'You've trained him well.'
>   Christopher laughed and said 'Yes.'
>   'Quite a little gent. And is this still his

china? You are a horror.'
   'That's his butter.'
He heard Elizabeth explode with laughter.
   'Well of all the—! It's too bad. He *must* be
a feeble sort of worm.'
   'Mother said he looked stuffed.'
   'Stuffed! That's *just* the word!'

John is far too absorbed in his fascination with the arrogant perfection of their middle-class living to resent what he has heard; so his perilous idolatry has to be converted into something more idealistic. His response is to create a private fantasy about a wholly invented sister at a boarding school in Derbyshire ('Willow Gables' also features in the title of 'an unclassifiable short story' which Larkin was writing during his Finals term: is this it?). And he proceeds not only to write the letters the imaginary Jill is supposed to have sent him, but also to compose her private journal and make her the main character in an elaborate girls' school story in the manner of Angela Brazil.

But then, to his amazement, he finds he has somehow spirited into existence a real Jill: she is a fifteen-year-old cousin of Elizabeth's, staying in Oxford with an aunt; and John must now pursue this evanescent bicycling vision through the streets of the city until he can initiate a relationship with her. The penalty he pays for this rash dreaming and sublimated class envy is a heavy one. Following Jill to an end-of-term party (drunk, and on his way there moving through a very curious and compelling *Walpurgisnacht* of undergraduate revels), he finally seizes and kisses her—and is dumped into an ice-cold fountain by roistering students. He finishes his first term in the college medical room, and we cannot see how he can recover enough personal dignity to start a second.

While there is a clear and obvious moral to be drawn here concerning the dangers of ordering one's existence according to private fantasies, a subtler point is made about the connection between desperate loneliness and the impulse to create. John Kemp is unconsciously transforming himself from the 'stuffed' and colourless being he was ('a mystery not worth solving') into a creative individual who will soon see beyond the 'invigorating' world of Christopher and his friends. As John writes about Jill in his social isolation we can already glimpse the lonely figure in some later Larkin poems who prefers creative or reflective solitude to enforced gregariousness (*'Dear Warlock-Williams/ I'm afraid—'*), though when this figure appears he is infinitely more capable than John Kemp of weighing the benefits of the games of loneliness against their risks. That John (so passive and lacking in 'luxuriance') could actually have written the highly assured and very enjoyable girls' school story pastiche is not strictly credible, but not a weakness in the novel. It is very credible indeed that he could have conceived the fantasies. The only disbelief we need to suspend is a lesser one: could he have *articulated* those fantasies to himself so explicitly in all that he writes about Jill? The convention that he could is not hard to accept.

Larkin has said about his poems that every one

> starts out as either true or beautiful. Then you try to make the true ones seem beautiful and the beautiful ones true.

John Kemp is striving to convert a balefully true world which is unfailingly destined to reject him into a beautiful dream of middle-class culture and manners, deriving from Jill. The story finely catches a particular sort of working-class envy of, and mistaken aspiration towards, that distant world. But *Jill* is much more than a sociological excursion. John's fantasies present a most delicate and abstract kind of erotic flight, peculiarly intense and coherent, and enthralling to follow, since Larkin also catches most details of the psychology of infatuation. John is in love with the imagined Jill (and the imagined qualities he implants in the real Jill) because she is himself: he has 'modelled himself on her image', much as he has wanted to achieve a brotherhood with Christopher.

Like John, the invented Jill is trapped in her isolation (at Willow Gables), and John's account of her own crush on a brilliant and lonely sixth-former takes us an important stage further into fantasies of desirable innocence. 'Minerva Strachey' (a very funny crossing of Bloomsbury, via a contemporary Labour politician, with the goddess of skilled crafts) is female, beautiful, public school *and* a university scholarship winner: 'To look at Minerva is like reading a page by a Stoic philosopher.' Moreover, she is delicately in charge of her own emotions when Jill makes an ill-judged gesture of friendship:

> Jill saw that Minerva had indicated that her detachment, even though it was admired, must still be respected; that loneliness was not to be abandoned at the first chance of friendship, but was a thing to be cherished in itself.

Even Minerva's loneliness, then, is a purification of the ploys of John's shabby isolation: his lonely wanderings in darkened Oxford streets, alongside water, among trees. Ordinary, plain miserable, rejection by a richer and faster world has been converted into a proud and brilliant solitude.

Anyone who knows the verse well can easily spot those moments when a Larkin poem, actual or imaginable, might be prised out: from the opening account of the train journey to Oxford ('The Whitsun Weddings'); in the observation of life lived either with reckless abandon (Christopher looks likely to shout 'Stuff your pension!') or with grubby self-interest (the student Whitbread in *Jill*, Arnold in 'Self's the Man'); in the descriptions of shoppers in the enclosed world of Oxford market (later they will recur in 'The Large Cool Store'); and in John's final perception that the real choices in life would be made (as in 'Dockery and Son') by something hidden from him:

> Let him take this course, or this course, but still behind the mind, on some other level, the way he had rejected was being simultaneously worked at and the same conclusion was being reached. What did it matter which road he took if they both led to the same place? He looked at the treetops in the wind. What control could he hope to have over the maddened surface of things?

Yet what finally impresses is not the signs of things to come in

Jill, but the conviction it carries as a novel about wartime Oxford
—wartime England—class, the springs of creativity and the
stratagems of erotic fantasy. The narrative develops with pace
and surprise; there is variety and confidence in the characteriza-
tion; and Larkin shows a near-infallible ear for dialogue on
several social levels. These are talents present, but not developed,
in *A Girl in Winter*.

The two novels do share one important feature: the war. And
Jill in fact deserves an honourable place in the fairly short list
of novels which accurately convey the feel of civilian life in
those years. The successfully evoked atmosphere of shabbiness
and shortage and the scenes in the bombed Huddlesford (based on
Larkin's witnessing of the devastation in Coventry in 1940) remind
us of stories by William Sansom or passages in novels by Henry
Green; but in neither instance does *Jill* suffer in the comparison.
Undergraduate life at Oxford in Michaelmas Term 1940 (ration-
books, tales of blitz experiences, friends dropping in from active
service) is a very precarious tenure of the opportunity for gam-
bling, drinking and womanizing. But Katherine Lind in *A Girl
in Winter* knows a more alarming sort of insecurity: as an alien in
a wartime provincial city, subject to police regulations, lonely
and friendless in her foreignness. The soured nature of the
present throws her holiday six years before, with a prosperous
English family in the Cotswolds, into a sharp and alluring
perspective.

At the beginning of *A Girl in Winter*, on a cold day waiting for
snow, we are in the cavernous, ill-heated branch library ruled by
Mr Anstey ('theatrical, scraggy and rude'). Katherine has found
employment there some months before (this is probably 1942),
but the sequence of events which has brought her to England
from her (unnamed) country of origin is never made exactly
clear. She is something of a ghostly visitant in this provincial
city, more than just a loner; all this is stranger, and vaguer, than
John Kemp's variety of social isolation. In this first of the novel's
three sections, there is an important thread of reference to
Katherine's earlier stay with her pen-friend Robin and his family.

She has just brought herself to write to Mrs Fennel, the mother of the family, and, knowing that she has passed on the letter to Robin, she waits anxiously on Robin's response. But the main plot line is concerned with Katherine's boredom and sense of humiliation in the library, and her relief at finding she can offer help and sympathy to *someone*, by taking a sick sixteen-year-old colleague to the dentist.

The prose of the book is precise and painstaking, with rather more of Virginia Woolf in it than any of the stylistic mannerisms of Henry Green. But there are surprises. Very little in *Jill*, or the earliest poems, would prepare a reader for Katherine's visit with Miss Green to the dental surgery. They find the dentist in dim and poky premises above the shops:

> he was a youngish man, but he had about him no youthful qualities. He wore spectacles and had pale blue eyes. His arms and shoulders were powerful, and he was dressed in a pale green sports coat buttoned closely and looking too small, and tubular flannel trousers. He half resembled an idiot boy whose body had developed at the expense of his mind.

The determined Katherine has to argue with him to obtain treatment, as he does not work on Saturdays and this is a Saturday morning. When he is finally persuaded, the operation moves to its climax with a striking, even a shocking, exactness of physical detail:

> It seemed impossible for the girl to feel nothing. As the dentist levered and wrenched again, the muscles in his wrist moved, and as he withdrew the forceps she thought he had failed until she saw the long root in their grip, bright with blood. He dropped it in a silver casket, then tweaked out the wet and bloodstained roll of cotton wool, and removed the rubber gag. . . . Katherine found that step by step she had moved right up to the very arm of the chair.

There is something of Graham Greene in this episode. But again one thinks first of later novelists: Stanley Middleton perhaps, David Storey. The raw impressiveness of the whole passage briefly suggests a development of Larkin's talents as a novelist in quite another direction.

But then the centre piece of the novel intervenes to carry Katherine back to her three-week holiday at the age of sixteen with Robin Fennel and his family (it is 1936, we infer: Katherine pins her brown tie with an Olympic badge). And the change is astonishing. The carefully crafted lyricism of this middle section works only too effectively to push *A Girl in Winter* towards that ideal of the sophisticated 'poetic' novel which Larkin apparently intended. The narrative of Katherine's journey from Dover to the elegant house in Oxfordshire, the account of her quiet holiday with Robin, the river trips and outings, Robin's kiss on the final evening—all this unfolds in a slow, deliberate idyll of a vanished past that seems more concerned with preserving the minutiae of Katherine's recollections than with advancing a plot. Time indeed seems to be 'passing slowly, luxuriously, like thick cream pouring from a silver jug'. Very gradually the holiday turns into something 'irrelevant and beautiful' and, above all, finished; like the love affair in poem XXX in *The North Ship*, something for the album alone:

> Cut, gummed; pastime of a provincial winter.

This is not a compelling process: the simplest risks of placing this aloof (and unexplained) young heroine in these unremarkable surroundings have not been avoided.

Yet there are some absorbing details. Larkin employs Katherine's innocent eye to define, in passing, certain traits and surfaces of Englishness which enter significantly into later poems. She is intrigued to hear, on the way to Oxfordshire. Robin's father lamenting the passing of the old rural England.

> it's the same all over England—good arable land being turned into pasture, pasture turning into housing estates. It'll be the ruin of us. . . . Suppose there's another war? What are we going to live on? Christmas crackers and ball bearings?

Later she goes with Robin and his sister Jane to a local gymkhana (it provides some of the liveliest passages in the section), a kind

of practice run for 'Show Saturday' in *High Windows*. 'It's strange
to me,'—she says—'It was very English and interesting.' But the
key passage in this connection is certainly Robin Fennel's account, 'speaking sincerely', of what his country really is, a modest
but very proud exposition for a foreign girl:

> Small fields, mainly pasture. Telegraph wires and a garage.
> That Empire Tea placard. And you know, don't you, that
> Britain is a small country, once agricultural but now highly
> industrialized, relying a great deal for food on a large Empire.
> You see, it all links up.

These ostensibly casual, unassuming limits set to a 'sincere'
definition of England certainly do link up—with the small and
cherished world which provides the landscape for the later
volumes of verse. By the 1970s, even the 'field and farms' are
'Going, Going' as this landscape turns into the 'First slum of
Europe'. But in 1947, and for some time yet, it's still a reasonably
proud setting for fiction and verse which simultaneously and
paradoxically celebrates 'the second best' (the late G. S. Fraser's
indispensable phrase about Larkin's area of reference)—and
splendidly transcends it.

In the third and last section of the novel we return to that
provincial winter of the first part. Robin Fennel has responded
to Katherine's letter by writing to say that he will be coming to
see her, on leave from the army, that very day. When Katherine
finally returns from the library to her lodgings, she discovers a
changed Robin waiting for her in the black-out: coarsened,
rather drunk, now bereft of the precocious social maturity he
displayed at sixteen; and eager to seduce her. At first she refuses
his approaches; but then, 'refusal would be dulling, an assent to
the wilderness that surrounded them'; and finally, almost in-
differently, she consents. It is an almost-instinct, a sense that what
may survive of this is indeed love. In bed, in the now snow-
covered city (the cold sometimes supplies a curiously affirmative
note in Larkin, not only the dowsing of a John Kemp in a fountain of reality), Robin muses on time, and human purpose, and on
the wry possibility of their marrying. The two of them fall asleep

with the dim, exhausted acknowledgement that the order, the destiny, in the hidden and inscrutable forces which govern their lives, may indeed be controlling things for the best. This is a moving and memorable ending, despite its ambiguities. And if the ending of 'An Arundel Tomb' is happy, so is that of *A Girl in Winter*.

This novel shares with *Jill* the theme of feeling one's way into an unfamiliar world. But Katherine Lind's experience is the more profoundly alarming, and the end of the novel resolves her dilemma more happily—more poignantly and skilfully—than the nasty conclusion of the first novel does John Kemp's. Yet *A Girl in Winter* still leaves an impression of unreal events happening within a framework of realism. Real, untidy experience seems to be gradually receding into the distance as the novel proceeds. The gentle ambivalence of Katherine's attitude to the Fennels and to her adopted English existence during the war is not quite enough of a theme to sustain interest.

In the last resort, the book somewhat resembles certain of those early Larkin poems in which the technique is already highly accomplished and the substance remains elusive. So it is fascinating indeed to wonder where that never-completed third novel might have taken him when we consider the poems that he was beginning to write in the late 1940s. Would it have returned to eligible areas of personal experience? Or would it (as seems more likely) have moved on into more rarefied places—were the worlds of Larkin's fiction and his poetry drawing slowly and irrevocably apart? Certainly to open *The Less Deceived* at 'Lines on a Young Lady's Photograph Album' is to discover at once something very different from Katherine Lind recalling an idealized past, or even stumbling upon an altered present. Another kind of figure, more humorous and more disconcerting, is looking over this young lady's shoulder, someone with a newly found confidence in another sort of personal voice. At some point a too-conscious quest for the beautiful in prose fiction, temporary and yet very powerful for Larkin, has finished; and the true is beginning to receive direct attention in the best English poetry of the post-war years.

Like Something Almost Being Said

CHRISTOPHER RICKS

'The whole frame of the poem', said Donne, 'is a beating out of a piece of gold, but the last clause is as the impression of the stamp, and that is it that makes it current.' Larkin's endings are finely judged, and so he proved a just judge of a poet—Emily Dickinson—who, like Donne, inaugurated poems magnificently: 'Only rarely, however, did she bring a poem to a successful conclusion: the amazing riches of originality offered by her index of first lines is belied on the page. . . . Too often the poem expires in a teased-out and breathless obscurity.' Larkin's poems do not expire. 'An Arundel Tomb' ends its volume, *The Whitsun Weddings*, and ends consummately. It is hard to say just where the ending begins. Not with the last line, which is ushered in by a colon. Not with the last sentence, which begins in mid-line, in the second line of the last stanza, and which anyway is an elucidation of the riddling half-a-dozen words which precede it. Not with the last stanza, which might well (less well) have been self-contained but is ushered in by its colon. Yet if you work back within the penultimate stanza, you find that again the sentence-shape is played against the stanza-shape: this sentence too begins in the stanza's second line, and it begins with 'Now', intimating a retrospect as well as a prospect. But if you work still further back, you find that the previous sentence begins with 'And'. And this would not provide the marked inauguration of an ending. . . . The poem speaks of prolonging, and is itself a tender prolongation. No stiffened pleats, no rigid persistence. In short, you cannot abbreviate the poem if you want to speak of its finality. Nevertheless:

> Time has transfigured them into
> Untruth. The stone fidelity
> They hardly meant has come to be
> Their final blazon, and to prove
> Our almost-instinct almost true:
> What will survive of us is love.

Love, not art, though it is art which tells us so.

The very last line has the apophthegmatic weight of classical art. Yet Larkin combines what in less good poets prove incompatible: the understandings both of classicism and of romanticism. It is a matter of tone, but the printed page, or rather the printed page of my discursive prose, is crude in its notation of intonations; it cannot but harden intimations into what Beckett, in *Company*, calls imperations: 'Same flat tone at all times. For its affirmations. For its negations. For its interrogations. For its exclamations. For its imperations. Same flat tone.' Still, to put it simply, Larkin's last line has at least two different possibilities of intonation. If you lay more weight on 'survive', you hear a classical asseveration—'What will *survive* of us is love'. Classical because what is meant by the less stressed 'us', taken in passing, is humanity at large, the largest community of all men and women; classical because of the transcending of individuality within commonalty. But the weight could, with equal propriety, be distributed differently; the words might be heard with more of their weight and salience devoted to 'us'—'What will survive of *us* is love'. This would be the weight of romantic apprehension; 'us', not as the unstressed and properly undifferentiated mankind, but as a particular 'us', here and now, moved not just personally but individually, particular visitors to a tomb or particular contemplators of one such visitor.

Romanticism's pathos of self-attention, its grounded pity for itself, always risks self-pity and soft warmth; classicism's stoicism, its grounded grief at the human lot, always risks frostiness. What Larkin achieves is an extraordinary complementarity; a classical pronouncement is protected against a carven coldness by the ghostly presence of an arching counterthrust, a romantic swell of feeling; and the romantic swell is protected against a melting self-solicitude by the bracing counterthrust of a classical impersonality. The classical intonation for the line says something *sotto voce*: 'What will survive—and not just mount, shine, evaporate, and fall—of us is love.' The romantic intonation says something different *sotto voce*: 'What will survive of us—of us too, ordinary modern people in an unarmorial age, uncommemorated by aristocratic art or by a Latin inscription—is love.'

Nothing could be more effortlessly direct than such a line as 'What will survive of us is love' (there is nothing disingenuous about the poem's introducing it with a colon), and yet the line is an axis, with two directions. The dignity and pathos of this line which opens out at the end of 'An Arundel Tomb' flow from its being strictly ineffable; you cannot simultaneously utter both of these intonations, though in uttering it—or in hearing it with an inner ear—with one of the intonations, you should comprehend that it might be otherwise uttered. If you were to stress both 'survive' and 'us', the line would not survive the plethora; and if you were to stress neither, the line would not survive the inanition. The line's compactness is that two lines, identical in wording but not in intonation, occupy exactly the same space.

> Nature that hateth emptiness,
> Allows of penetration less.
> ('An Horatian Ode')

The penetration of Marvell's poetry was at one with its duality of wit, and there is a sombre wit in Larkin's line, wit as most comprehensively defined by T. S. Eliot in speaking of Marvell: 'It involves, probably, a recognition, implicit in the expression of every experience, of other kinds of experience which are possible.' The dignity of such wit comes from its conceding that the possibilities cannot all be made simultaneously explicit and yet that the magnanimous imagination can grant their existence; the pathos comes from the acknowledgement that we can entertain the thought of such a universal realm but cannot enter the realm itself.

> The trees are coming into leaf
> Like something almost being said. . . .

There is many a way in which things may almost be said. Absences, as in Larkin's poem of that title, make themselves felt; and 'Maiden Name' ends with a line the obvious rhyme for which has not been granted but left unsounded, silently wedded: 'With your depreciating luggage laden'. As with so much of Larkin, the art is a version of pastoral, an apprehension of poignant contraries. The last line of 'An Arundel Tomb' functions as an inscription itself, lucid and gnomic, an oracular and honourable equivocation, its possibilities equally voiced. Like the Latin inscription spoken of within the poem, it entails some contrariety of looking and reading. The earl and countess would not have imagined the swift decay of the international language of commemoration: 'How soon succeeding eyes begin/ To look, not read'.

Larkin's classical temper shows its mettle when he deplores modernism, whether in jazz, poetry, or painting: 'I dislike such things not because they are new, but because they are irresponsible exploitations of technique in contradiction of human life as we know it. This is my essential criticism of modernism, whether perpetrated by Parker, Pound or Picasso: it helps us neither to enjoy nor endure.' Dr Johnson compacted classicism into the confidence that men more often require to be reminded than informed, and it was Dr Johnson of whom Larkin reminded us when he said that modernism 'helps us neither to enjoy nor endure'. 'The only end of writing is to enable the readers better to enjoy life or better to endure it.' Yet though Larkin's convictions are classical, his impulses are romantic; as in a great deal of romantic poetry, self-pity is a central concern and has to be watched lest it become the dominant impulse. The argument about Larkin is essentially as to whether his poems are given up to self-pity or given to a scrutiny of self-pity and in particular to an alert refusal of easy disparaging definitions of it. If we should love our neighbour as ourselves, why should we not be permitted to feel as sorry for ourselves as for our neighbour?

The objection to Shelley's torrid cry, 'I fall upon the thorns of life! I bleed!', is that it would sound coolly unconcerned if it were transposed to the third person plural: 'They fall upon the thorns of life! They bleed!' *Tiens*. Whereas the triumph of Larkin's ending to 'Afternoons' is that, though it is specifically about the young mothers and has no *œillade* of mirrored self-attention, it yet would not be an embarrassing or self-pitying reflection if it were turned to the first person.

> Their beauty has thickened.
> Something is pushing them
> To the side of their own lives.

To grow old is to be pushed to the side of your own life; something pushes all of us there, yet the somethings are different. The life to which you have given birth, a child, is a manifest and embodied something which pushes you to the side of your own life. But then your poem might push you there too. There is no sense of grievance or of being victimized, simply a flat fidelity. So if we were to transpose it into either a larger commonalty, with 'them' meaning not only young mothers but all of us, the poem's way of speaking would be large enough to accommodate this; or if we were to imagine the 'them' contracted into any single one of us— 'Something is pushing me/ To the side of my own life'—Larkin's way of speaking would be strict enough, calm enough, to acknowledge the pity of it. The poetry is in the pity, for oneself no less than for others.

> *Poor soul,*
> They whisper at their own distress. . . .
> ('Ambulances')

At, not *to*, though it is to their distress that they are moved to whisper.

Larkin's responsible control of tone includes the delegation of responsibility. In responses begin responsibilities, and the recognition, implicit in the expression of every experience, of other kinds of experience which are possible, informs Larkin's belief that for his poetry of lyric meditation the proper medium is the printed page, since there the words are not pressed to the either/ or of utterance. The poet who wrote 'The Importance of Elsewhere' is alive to the importance of elsehow—a word from elsewhen which should not have been let die. Wittgenstein's duck/rabbit cannot simultaneously be seen as a duck and as a rabbit, however fast we click our focusing; yet it can be known to be also the other even while it is being seen as the one. What is a perceptual or philosophical trick or flick becomes in Larkin this version of pastoral. Hence Larkin's greatest soft sell, when he did his best to discourage prospective purchasers of his recording of *The Whitsun Weddings*; the form which solicited your order included Larkin's rumbling comedy:

> And what you gain on the sound you lose on the sense: think of all the mishearings, the 'their' and 'there' confusions, the submergence of rhyme, the disappearance of stanza-shape, even the comfort of knowing how far you are from the end!

For the sense of nearing a destination, something which is apprehended by sight quite differently from hearing, and which itself arrives at one of Larkin's great destinations, the end of 'The Whitsun Weddings': this sense is more than a comfort; it is a shaping spirit of imagination. Indeed, it is one of the paradoxes and strengths of his art that it is at once diversely idiomatic and yet in some crucial respects cannot be voiced at all. When a poetry-speaker on the BBC ushers in a poem by saying '1914', you sympathize, since some title has to be given and he couldn't say 'MCMXIV'. Yet how much of the sense of loss is lost. How long the continuity was with ancient wars and with immemorial commemoration; how sharp is the passing of an era. 'Never such innocence again'.

Tact is necessary but insufficient, since there may still be an irreducible other sounding. The movement of a poem like 'Going, Going' ('Gone' has not gone, but will come soon, sadly) is one which gives a particular hinged stress to these lines:

> For the first time I feel somehow
> That it isn't going to last. . . .

For the stress has to go, delicately, on 'isn't', not exactly where it would have gone if the lines had not been anticipated within the poem. 'That it *isn't*—contrary to what I had thought—going to last'. For more than thirty lines earlier, the poem had kicked off with: 'I thought it would last my time'; and we find that we needed to carry responsibly and lastingly forward the memory of that launching, that attractive and good-humoured irresponsibility, so that this might brace the later moment with a salutary recognition, now that the crucial word 'last' (coming for the second time) demands the strongly conceded stress on 'isn't':

> For the first time I feel somehow
> That it isn't going to last. . . .

The poem is going to.

It is a corollary that the moment at which a Larkin poem loses hold is likely to be one when a reader cannot make sense and sensibility of the relation between repetition and intonation. As, for me, just before the end of 'The Whitsun Weddings'. The newly-weds watched the landscape:

> —and none
> Thought of the others they would never meet
> Or how their lives would all contain this hour.
> I thought of London spread out in the sun,
> Its postal districts packed like squares of wheat:

I don't know how the man knows that none of them thought those things (and yet this itself doesn't seem to be up for scrutiny within the poem), and my unease is accentuated by my not being able to hear the relation between 'none thought' and 'I thought'. None thought this whereas I thought it, or whereas I thought something quite other? If there is no stress placed upon 'I' in 'I thought', the hinge turns idly; but if 'I' is at all stressed, what depends from the hinge? Pronouns, especially in their both contrasting and assimilating 'I' and others, are asked to take such weight in Larkin's poems that any factitious relationship (none thought/I thought?) does real damage.

The very structure of a poem like 'Mr Bleaney' turns upon the decision as to the precise degree of stress and precisely where to lay it. Once the speaker (so to speak) takes Mr Bleaney's place, the shape of the poem is simple: 'I know his habits' (this and that), and 'their yearly frame' (this, that, and the other):

> But if he stood and watched the frigid wind
> Tousling the clouds, lay on the fusty bed
> Telling himself that this was home, and grinned,
> And shivered, without shaking off the dread
>
> That how we live measures our own nature,
> And at his age having no more to show
> Than one hired box should make him pretty sure
> He warranted no better, I don't know.

But if he stood, as I do, and . . .: the plot of the poem asks some stress on *he*; and yet it is a stress that becomes increasingly and illuminatingly difficult to maintain with grace and exactitude as the final eight-line sentence rolls on. 'Telling *him*self'—as I tell *my*self: the antithesis-cum-assimilation may still be pointed up by the voice, but by the time we reach 'at his age', and 'make him pretty sure', and 'he warranted', the contrastive *I* has been dissolved to wan wistlessness. At which point 'I' makes itself heard: 'I don't know'. But to accentuate this other arch of the structure (I know his habits, but these things I *don't* know) by coming down unignorably on 'don't' would be as coarsening as it would be to slight this structural turn.

Without the contrast furnished by 'I know his habits', there would be at the end a more mild puzzlement, equalizing the stresses within 'I don't know'; and this puzzlement must not be sacrificed to the more urgent fears (was he just like me? am I just like him?), since these last eight lines subtly twine an ordinary wondering and a morbid anxiety. Is the speaker imputing his own sensitivities and anxieties to Mr Bleaney, or is he acknowledging a true fellow-feeling? Any act of imagination risks the accusation that it is just an imputing of oneself, a sort of anthropomorphism, but then is this accusation too an unimaginative imputation? 'I don't know.' You must stress to some degree all three of those concluding words; yet you mustn't treat 'don't' as if it were not an unpriceable pivot. But then nor must you slight the first of persons, 'I', or the searching verb 'know'. 'Mr Bleaney' is one of Larkin's best poems, and it is natural that it should come to its consummation of 'incomplete unrest' with those three words: the pronoun which so often marks the crucial turn or takes the crucial stress in his poetry; the colloquial negative 'don't'; and the admission as to doubtful knowledge.

'Know' can function similarly at the start of a poem, as with 'Ignorance', where the first words might advance naturally towards a stress on nothing—'Strange to know *nothing*'—only then to be retrospectively reconsidered because of being followed by 'never to be sure/ Of what is true or right or real'. For the succession asks that there be a stronger stress on 'know' than you could have known at the time:

> Strange to know nothing, never to be sure
> Of what is true or right or real,
> But forced to qualify *or so I feel*. . . .

An equal stress on 'I' and 'feel'?

The start of 'Toads' offers a pronominal prospect which is likewise qualified as the poem moves on:

> Why should I let the toad *work*
> Squat on my life?

The general aggrievedness, which is at first all there is to go on, would stress 'should'—'Why *should* I?'. But it then turns out, as things continue, that there is a particular aggrievedness instead or as well, which means: 'Why should *I*, who am no fool, let the toad work squat on *my* life?' You can feel these challenging undulations of tone, idiomatic and yet unspeakable, in a stanza like this:

> Their nippers have got bare feet,
> Their unspeakable wives
> Are skinny as whippets—and yet
> No one actually *starves*.

On Hull Corporation Pier, 1974

Drawing by Howard Morgan, in the possession of the University of Hull, 1979

This needs both the tone of matter-of-fact reportage, without argumentative stresses until the last word, and the pitching upon 'have' and 'Are' which will bring out the concessive combativeness: 'True, their nippers *have* got bare feet, and their unspeakable wives *are*—oh yes—skinny as whippets—and yet. . . .' Larkin's accents are audible either as equable or as elbowing.

'Unspeakable': negative prefixes matter to Larkin for what they cannot but call up, and an unspoken but not unheard melody is one of his honest insinuations. The negative prefix may be markedly absent, as when Larkin musically imagines 'Mute glorious Storyvilles' ('For Sidney Bechet') challenging us to sound the mute prefix *in-*—or at least not to succumb to merely hitting upon 'glorious' as if this would make music or sense. Allusion like this (double or triple, since it plays upon Gray as well as upon Milton) always invites at least two effects of intonation: the voice must use its pitch so that it gives one kind of salience to the words that have been carried over unchanged, and it must use its stress so that it gives a different kind of salience to the words that have been changed and that therefore constitute the narrative of the matter. The opening of Edmund Blunden's best poem, 'Report on Experience', would not be sounded in the same way if it were not that the Psalmist were audible.

> I have been young, and now am not too old,
> And I have seen the righteous forsaken. . . .

'I have been young, and now am old: and yet saw I never the righteous forsaken. . . .' So the tones of Blunden's lines must be something like this:

> *I* have been young, and now am *not too* 'old'
> And I *have* 'seen the righteous forsaken'. . . .

A characteristic Larkin turn of phrase like 'the wind's incomplete unrest' ('Talking in Bed') alludes to the easy restfulness of the phrase 'a complete rest'—a phrase newly completed unrestfully. But uttering this—saying the words, as against imagining them—is not as easy as it sounds. If you stress the negative prefixes, '*in*complete *un*rest', you reduce the effect to that of a dig in the ribs; but if you don't stress them at all, you cut free from the tacit down-to-earth idiom which touchingly tethers the high fancy. Again, it is commonplace to meet a welcome and easily said, but how do you say 'Meet a vast unwelcome ('First Sight')? It asks a stress small enough to be no strain. Or there is the negative prefix at the very end of 'Spring': 'Their visions mountain-clear, their needs immodest'. Our modest needs are one thing; our immodest needs would be something other than quite other, since immodest isn't exactly the opposite of modest. Yet the alighting upon the negative prefix must be delicate—must meet the modest needs of such exact art. Likewise with the felicity which ends a poem ('Wild Oats') with the line 'Unlucky charms, perhaps'. To stress the prefix would be to smirk, and to ignore it would be to wear a vacant look. Larkin's art is varying and almost invariably lovely, and a phrase like 'Unvariably lovely there' ('Lines on a Young Lady's Photograph Album') depends on 'unvariably' being a variation of the usual 'invariably', from which it differs as minutely and substantially as does T. S. Eliot's 'unsubstantial' ('Are become unsubstantial', in 'Marina') from 'insubstantial'. Larkin's too is a poetry in which things both great and small shine substantially expressed.

The Main of Light

SEAMUS HEANEY

E. M. Forster once said that he envisaged *A Passage to India* as a
book with a hole in the middle of it. I have often thought that
some poems are like that too, having openings at their imaginative
centre that take the reader through and beyond. Shakespeare's
Sonnet 60, for example:

> Like as the waves make towards the pebbled shore,
> So do our minutes hasten to their end;
> Each changing place with that which goes before,
> In sequent toil all forwards do contend.
> Nativity, once in the main of light,
> Crawls to maturity, wherewith being crowned,
> Crooked eclipses 'gainst his glory fight,
> And Time that gave doth now his gift confound.

Something visionary happens there in the fifth line. 'Nativity' sets
up a warning tremor just before the mind's eye is dazzled by 'the
main of light', and for a split second we are in the world of the
Paradiso. The rest of the poem lives melodiously in a world of
discourse but it is this successful strike into the realm of pure
being that marks the sonnet with Shakespeare's extravagant genius.

In so far as it is a poem alert to the sadness of life's changes but
haunted too by a longing for some adjacent 'pure serene', the
sonnet rehearses in miniature the whole poignant score of Philip
Larkin's poetry. With Larkin, we respond constantly to the melody of intelligence, to a verse that is as much commentary as it
is presentation, and it is this encounter between a compassionate,

unfoolable mind and its own predicaments—which we are forced to recognize as our predicaments too—that gives his poetry its first appeal. Yet while Larkin is exemplary in the way he sifts the conditions of contemporary life, refuses alibis and pushes consciousness towards an exposed condition that is neither cynicism nor despair, there survives in him a repining for a more crystalline reality to which he might give allegiance. When that repining finds expression something opens and moments occur which deserve to be called visionary. Because he is suspicious of any easy consolation, he is sparing of such moments, yet when they come they stream into the discursive and exacting world of his poetry with such trustworthy force that they call for attention.

In his introduction to the reissue of *The North Ship*, Larkin recalls a merry and instructive occasion during the period of his infatuation with Yeats. 'I remember Bruce Montgomery snapping, as I droned for the third or fourth time that evening *When such as I cast out remorse, so great a sweetness flows into the breast . . .*, "It's not his job to cast off remorse, but to earn forgiveness." But then Bruce Montgomery had known Charles Williams.' Larkin tells the anecdote to illustrate his early surrender to Yeats's music and also to commend the anti-romantic, morally sensitive attitude which Montgomery was advocating and which would eventually issue in his conversion to the poetry of Thomas Hardy. Yet it also illustrates that appetite for sweetness flowing into the breast, for the sensation of revelation, which I believe has never deserted him. Indeed the exchange between Montgomery and himself prefigures the shape of the unsettled quarrel conducted all through the mature poetry between vision and experience. And if that anti-heroic, chastening, humanist voice is the one which is allowed most of the lines throughout the later poetry, the rebukes it delivers cannot quite banish the Yeatsian need for a flow of sweetness.

That sweetness flows most reliably into the poetry as a stream of light. In fact, there is something Yeatsian in the way that Larkin, in *High Windows*, places his sun poem immediately after and in answer to his moon poem: 'Sad Steps' and 'Solar' face each other on the opened page like the two halves of his poetic personality in dialogue. In 'Sad Steps' the wary intelligence is tempted by a moment of lunar glamour. The renaissance moon of Sidney's sonnet sails close, and the invitation to yield to the 'enormous yes' that love should evoke is potent, even for a man who has just taken a piss:

> I part thick curtains, and am startled by
> The rapid clouds, the moon's cleanliness.
>
> Four o'clock: wedge-shadowed gardens lie
> Under a cavernous, a wind-picked sky.

His vulnerability to desire and hope are transmitted in the Tennysonian cadence of that last line and a half, but suddenly the delved brow tightens—'There's something laughable about this' —only to be tempted again by a dream of fullness, this time in the symbolist transports of language itself—'O wolves of memory, immensements!' But, of course, he finally comes out with a definite, end-stopped 'No'. Truth wins over beauty by a few points, and while the appeal of the poem lies in its unconsoled clarity about the seasons of ageing, our nature still tends to run to fill that symbolist hole in the middle.

However, the large yearnings that are kept firmly in their rational place in 'Sad Steps' are given scope to 'climb and return like angels' in 'Solar'. This is frankly a prayer, a hymn to the sun, releasing a generosity that is in no way attenuated when we look twice and find that the praise could be as phallic as it is solar. Where the moon is 'preposterous and separate,/ Lozenge of love! Medallion of art!', described in the language of the ironical, emotionally defensive man, the sun is a 'lion face', 'an origin', a 'petalled head of flames', 'unclosing like a hand', all phrases of candid feeling. The poem is most unexpected and daring, close to the pulse of primitive poetry, unprotected by any sleight of tone or persona. The poet is bold to stand uncovered in the main of light, far from the hatless one who took off his cycle-clips in awkward reverence:

SEAMUS HEANEY

> Coined there among
> Lonely horizontals
> You exist openly.
> Our needs hourly
> Climb and return like angels.
> Unclosing like a hand
> You give forever

These are the words of someone surprised by 'a hunger in himself to be more serious', though there is nothing in the poem, of course, that the happy atheist could not accept. Yet in the angels simile and in the generally choral tone of the whole thing, Larkin opens stops that he usually cares to keep muted, stops which are nevertheless vital to the power and purity of his work.

'Deceptions', for example, seems to me to depend upon a bright, still centre for its essential poetic power. Already the image of a window rises to take in the facts of grief, to hold them at bay and in focus. The violated girl's mind lies open 'like a drawer of knives' and most of the first stanza registers the dead-still sensitivity of the gleaming blades to the changing moods of the afternoon light. What we used to consider in our Christian Doctrine classes under the heading of 'the mystery of suffering' becomes actual in the combined sensations of absolute repose and trauma, made substantial in images that draw us into a raw identification with the girl:

> The sun's occasional print, the brisk brief
> Worry of wheels along the street outside
> Where bridal London bows the other way,
> And light, unanswerable and tall and wide,
> Forbids the scar to heal, and drives
> Shame out of hiding. All the unhurried day
> Your mind lay open like a drawer of knives.

It is this light-filled dilation at the heart of the poem which transposes it from lament to comprehension and prepares the way for the sharp irony of the concluding lines. I have no doubt that Larkin would repudiate any suggestion that the beauty of the

lines I have quoted is meant to soften the pain, as I have no doubt
he would also repudiate the Pedlar's advice to Wordsworth in
'The Ruined Cottage' where, having told of the long sufferings of
Margaret, he bids the poet 'be wise and cheerful'. And yet the
Pedlar's advice arises from his apprehension of 'an image of
tranquillity' that works in much the same way as the Larkin
passage:

> those very plumes,
> Those weeds, and the high spear grass on that wall,
> By mist and silent raindrops silvered o'er.

It is the authenticity of this moment of pacification which to some
extent guarantees the Pedlar's optimism and in a similar way the
blank tenderness at the heart of Larkin's poem takes it beyond
irony and bitterness, though keeping it short of facile consolation: 'I would not dare/ Console you if I could'.

Since Larkin is a poet as explicit as he is evocative, it is no
surprise to find him coining terms that describe exactly the kind
of effect I am talking about: 'Here', the first poem in *The Whitsun
Weddings*, ends by defining it as a sense of 'unfenced existence'
and by supplying the experience that underwrites that spacious
abstraction:

> Here silence stands
> Like heat. Here leaves unnoticed thicken,
> Hidden weeds flower, neglected waters quicken,
> Luminously-peopled air ascends;
> And past the poppies bluish neutral distance
> Ends the land suddenly beyond a beach
> Of shapes and shingle. Here is unfenced existence:
> Facing the sun, untalkative, out of reach.

It is a conclusion that recalls the conclusion of Joyce's 'The Dead'
—and indeed *Dubliners* is a book very close to the spirit of
Larkin, whose collected work would fit happily under the title
Englanders. It is an epiphany, an escape from the 'scrupulous
meanness' of the disillusioned intelligence, and we need only
compare 'Here' with 'Show Saturday', another poem that seeks

its form by an accumulation of detail, to see how vital to the
success of 'Here' is this gesture towards a realm beyond the social
and the historical. 'Show Saturday' remains encumbered in
naturalistic data, and while its conclusion beautifully expresses the
nostalgic patriotism that is also an important part of this poet's
make-up, the note is less one of plangent vision, more a matter
of liturgical wishfulness: 'Let it always be so'.

'If I were called in/ To construct a religion/ I should make use
of water'—but he could make use of 'Here' as well; and 'Solar';
and 'High Windows'; and 'The Explosion'; and 'Water', the
poem from which the lines are taken. It is true that the jaunty
tone of these lines and the downbeat vocabulary later on of
'sousing,/ A furious devout drench,' are indicative of Larkin's
unease with the commission he has imagined for himself. But just
as 'Solar' and 'Here' yield up occasions where 'unfenced existence' can, without embarrassment to the sceptical man, find space
to reveal its pure invitations, so too 'Water' escapes from its
man-of-the-world nonchalance into a final stanza which is held
above the rest of the poem like a natural monstrance:

> And I should raise in the east
> A glass of water
> Where any-angled light
> Would congregate endlessly.

The minute light makes its presence felt in Larkin's poetry; he
cannot resist the romantic poet in himself who must respond with
pleasure and alacrity, exclaiming, as it were, 'Already with thee!'
The effects are various but they are all extraordinary, from the
throwaway surprises of 'a street/ Of blinding windscreens' or 'the
differently-swung stars' or 'that high-builded cloud/ Moving at
summer's pace' to the soprano delights of this stanza from 'An
Arundel Tomb':

> Snow fell, undated. Light
> Each summer thronged the glass. A bright
> Litter of bird-calls strewed the same
> Bone-riddled ground. And up the paths
> The endless altered people came,

and from that restraint to the manic spasm in this, from 'Livings,
II':

> Guarded by brilliance
> I set plate and spoon,
> And after, divining-cards,
> Lit shelved liners
> Grope like mad worlds westward.

The resource is astonishing. Light, so powerfully associated with
joyous affirmation, is even made to serve a ruthlessly geriatric
vision of things in 'The Old Fools':

> Perhaps being old is having lighted rooms
> Inside your head, and people in them, acting.

And it is refracted even more unexpectedly at the end of 'High
Windows' when one kind of brightness, the brightness of belief
in liberation and amelioration, falls from the air which immediately fills with a different, infinitely neutral splendour:

> And immediately
>
> Rather than words comes the thought of high windows:
> The sun-comprehending glass,
> And beyond it, the deep blue air, that shows
> Nothing, and is nowhere, and is endless.

All these moments spring from the deepest strata of Larkin's
poetic self, and they are connected with another kind of mood
that pervades his work and which could be called elysian: I am
thinking in particular of poems like 'At Grass', 'MCLMXIV',
'How Distant' and, most recently, 'The Explosion'. To borrow
Geoffrey Hill's borrowing from Coleridge, these are visions of
'the old Platonic England', the light in them honeyed by attach-
ment to a dream world that will not be denied because it is at the
foundation of the poet's sensibility. It is the light that was on
Langland's Malvern, 'in summer season, when soft was the sun',
at once local and timeless. In 'The Explosion' the field full of folk
has become a coalfield and something Larkin shares with his
miners 'breaks ancestrally . . . into/ Regenerate union'.

The dead go on before us, they
Are sitting in God's house in comfort,
We shall see them face to face

Plain as lettering in the chapels
It was said, and for a second
Wives saw men of the explosion

Larger than in life they managed—
Gold as on a coin, or walking
Somehow from the sun towards them,

One showing the eggs unbroken.

If Philip Larkin were ever to compose his version of *The Divine Comedy* he would probably discover himself not in a dark wood but in a railway tunnel half-way on a journey down England. His inferno proper might occur before dawn, as a death-haunted aubade, whence he might emerge into the lighted room inside the head of an old fool, and then his purgatorial ascent would be up through the 'lucent comb' of some hospital building where men in hired boxes would stare out at a wind-tousled sky. We have no doubt about his ability to recount the troubles of such souls who walk the rising ground of 'extinction's alp'. His disillusioned compassion for them has been celebrated and his need to keep numbering their griefs has occasionally drawn forth protests that he narrows the possibilities of life so much that the whole earth is a hospital. I want to suggest that Larkin also has it in him to write his own version of the *Paradiso*. It might well amount to no more than an acknowledgement of the need to imagine 'such attics cleared of me, such absences'; nevertheless, in the poems he has written there is enough reach and longing to show that he does not completely settle for that well-known bargain offer, 'a poetry of lowered sights and patently diminished expectations'.

Going to Parties

for Philip Larkin

PETER PORTER

Truth to experience, to the sombre facts,
    We all believe in;
That men get overtaken by their acts,
That the randy and highminded both inherit
Space enough for morals to conceive in
    And prove the pitch of merit:
Such insight hangs upon the scraping pen
Of the deep-browed author writing after ten.

But there behind him, if he chose to look,
    The ranks of those
Whose sheerest now is always in a book
Are closing; yes, he's broken up some ground;
It lies about in other people's prose,
    Great graces that abound—
Meanwhile, incorrigibly, people seem
To write their own existence from a dream.

Perhaps it makes him think of earlier days
    When parties beckoned,
Quartz studs glittering in a bank of clays,
And he'd set out, though apprehensive,
Hoping this time to come in first, not second,
    Ready to really live,
Only to find that life which offers chances
Ignores the sitters-out and picks the dancers.

Yet he got something there. How to enjoy
 Expansive moments,
How it must stun the gods to be a boy
Who will not bear the cup, how unasked
Guests act prosecution and defence
 (Who was the man in the mask?),
And how exhilarating when alone
To know those dandies walk on stilts of bone.

Tributes then; the party isn't over,
 A few guests linger.
From heartland England on to distant Dover
People are shutting doors they know too well
And following their feet to hope, the bringer
 Of several shapes of Hell,
Of time, experience, and all we use
To make art of a life we didn't choose.

Archibald

for Philip Larkin

JOHN BETJEMAN

The bear who sits above my bed
  An agéd bear he is to see,
From out his drooping pear-shaped head
  His woollen eyes look into me.
He has no mouth, but seems to say:
  'They'll burn you on the Judgment Day.'

Those woollen eyes, the things they've seen;
  Those flannel ears, the things they've heard—
Among horse-chestnut fans of green,
  The fluting of an April bird,
And quarrelling downstairs until
  Doors slammed at Thirty One West Hill.

The dreaded evening keyhole scratch
  Announcing some return below,
The nursery landing's lifted latch,
  The punishment to undergo—
Still I could smooth those half-moon ears
  And wet that forehead with my tears.

Whatever rush to catch a train,
  Whatever joy there was to share
Of sounding sea-board, rainbowed rain,
  Or seaweed-scented Cornish air,
Still you were there, the laughs to share,
  You ugly, unrepentant bear.

When nine, I hid you in a loft
    And dared not let you share my bed;
My father would have thought me soft,
    Or so at least my mother said.
She only then our secret knew,
    And thus my guilty passion grew.

The bear who sits above my bed
    More agéd now he is to see,
His woollen eyes have thinner thread,
    But still he seems to say to me,
In double-doom notes, like a knell:
    'You're half a century nearer Hell.'

Self-pity shrouds me in a mist,
    And drowns me in my self-esteem.
The freckled faces I have kissed
    Float by me in a guilty dream.
The only constant, sitting there,
    Patient and hairless, is a bear.

And if an analyst one day
    Of school of Adler, Jung or Freud
Should take this agéd bear away,
    Then, Oh my God, the dreadful void!
Its draughty darkness could but be
    Eternity, Eternity.

An Old Larkinian

GAVIN EWART

When I think of the crumby poetry
   people turn out to honour some pseuds
and Old Pretenders (and you must know it!)—*re*
   Art, alas, there are always such feuds—
so many whom Kingsley would simply call shags
or, if female, could be regarded as hags
   or old bags,

are enshrined in collectors' items, *Festschriften,*
   that others think give verse a bad name!
So it's like taking sides, saying 'I was at Clifton'
   or 'I'm an Etonian', no one can blame
poets for being admirers well-versed in one another
like a worshipping schoolboy younger brother
   or a mother

proud of the son's or daughter's achievements,
   sticking the pins of the journey into the map,
following them through loves and bereavements,
   seeing them off each morning in a school cap,
more than terribly pleased when they make the team,
celebrating the Knighthood with a joyful scream;
   a sunbeam

indeed he seems, or she! I'm a Larkinian
   and glad to acknowledge it to all;

though I know that death has a lot of dominion
  my admiration for your verse is not small,
you are far the best of the lonely scullers
and I'm proud to wear, among solemners and dullers,
  your colours.

Notes on Contributors

ANTHONY THWAITE was born in 1930 and read English at Christ Church, Oxford. He has taught in universities in Japan and Libya, worked as a BBC radio producer and as literary editor in turn of the *Listener* and the *New Statesman*, and since 1973 has been co-editor of *Encounter*. His seven books of poetry include *A Portion for Foxes* (1977) and *Victorian Voices* (1980).

NOEL HUGHES was born in 1921, was at King Henry VIII School, Coventry, St John's College, Oxford, and the London School of Economics, and was at one time special correspondent of *The Times* on higher education and editor of its supplement *Technology*. Subsequently he became a publisher, and was a director of Associated Book Publishers Ltd and managing director of Chapman & Hall and other publishers. He has now resigned, and describes his interests as 'a Thames skiff, making stringed instruments and eastern Christianity'.

KINGSLEY AMIS was born in 1922, was at St John's College, Oxford, and formerly lectured in English at Swansea University and Peterhouse, Cambridge. His many novels range from *Lucky Jim* (1954) to *Russian Hide and Seek* (1980). His *Collected Poems 1944–1979* were published in 1979.

ROBERT CONQUEST was born in 1917, was at Magdalen College, Oxford, and for some years worked in the Foreign Office. He has published several books of poems (most recently *Forays*, 1979), edited *New Lines* and *New Lines II*, and has also published books on history and politics, notably *The Great Terror* (1968).

CHARLES MONTEITH was born in 1921, was at Magdalen College, Oxford, and is a Fellow of All Souls College, Oxford. He joined Faber & Faber in 1953, became a Director in 1954, and from 1976 until 1981 was Chairman. Since then he has been Senior Editorial Consultant.

B. C. BLOOMFIELD was born in 1931, was at the universities of Exeter and London, and is the Director of the India Office Library and Records, Foreign and Commonwealth Office. His bibliography of W. H. Auden was published in 1964 (second edition, with Edward Mendelson, 1972). Faber & Faber published his bibliography of Philip Larkin in 1979.

DOUGLAS DUNN was born in 1942 in Scotland, trained as a librarian, and later took a First in English at Hull University. He is now a freelance writer. He has published five books of poems, beginning with *Terry Street* (1969), and most recently *St Kilda's Parliament* (1981).

HARRY CHAMBERS was born in 1937 and took his degree in English at Liverpool University. He founded the magazine *Phoenix* (which ran from 1959 to 1975 and published a special Philip Larkin issue in 1974), and also his own publishing firm, Peterloo Poets. After several years lecturing in colleges of education, since 1977 he has lived and worked in Cornwall.

ANDREW MOTION was born in 1952, was at University College, Oxford, and was a lecturer in English at Hull University, from which he took a year's unpaid leave of absence in 1980–1 in order to write. He published his first book of poems, *The Pleasure Steamers*, in 1978, and won the first prize of £5000 in the 1980 Arvon Foundation/*Observer* national poetry competition. He has also published a book on Edward Thomas.

ALAN BENNETT was born in 1934 in Leeds, and read history at Exeter College, Oxford. He was co-author of and acted in *Beyond the Fringe*, and since then his many stage and television plays have included *Forty Years On, Getting On, Habeas Corpus, The Old Country,* and *Enjoy.*

DONALD MITCHELL was born in 1925, was a member of the music staff of the *Daily Telegraph* 1959–64, Professor of Music at Sussex University 1971–6, and is now chairman of Faber Music Ltd and Director of Academic Studies at the Britten–Pears School for Advanced Musical Studies. His books include *The Language of Modern Music*, a study of the collaboration between Britten and Auden, and a study of Mahler. He will be writing the authorized biography of Britten.

JOHN GROSS was born in 1935, was at Wadham College, Oxford, lectured in English at Queen Mary College, London, and King's College, Cambridge, and worked for a time in publishing. He was formerly literary editor of the *New Statesman*, and from 1974 to 1981 was editor of *The Times Literary Supplement.* He is now deputy chairman of Weidenfeld and Nicolson. Among his books are *The Rise and Fall of the Man of Letters* (1969).

GEORGE HARTLEY was born in 1933, and founded the magazine *Listen* in Hessle, near Hull, in 1953. He also founded the Marvell Press there, which in the 1950s published Larkin's *The Less Deceived*, John Holloway's *The Moment*, Donald Davie's *Forests of Lithuania*, Anthony Thwaite's *Home Truths*, and several other books of poems.

CLIVE JAMES was born in 1939 in Australia, took his first degree at Sydney University, and then emigrated to Britain in 1962, where he took another degree at Cambridge. He is television critic of the *Observer*, and has published two collections of his columns there, a volume of autobiography (*Unreliable Memoirs*, 1980), a book of verse letters, four satirical 'verse epics', and two collections of criticism, most recently *At the Pillars of Hercules* (1978).

ALAN BROWNJOHN was born in 1931, was at Merton College, Oxford, where he read history, and taught in various schools and colleges of education until he became a freelance writer. The most recent of his seven books of poems are *A Song of Good Life* (1975) and *A Night in the Gazebo* (1980). His short study of Larkin in the British Council 'Writers and their Work' series was published by Longmans in 1975.

CHRISTOPHER RICKS was born in 1933, was at Balliol College, Oxford, and was formerly a Fellow of Worcester College, Oxford, and Professor of English at Bristol University. Since 1975 he has been Professor of English at Cambridge University. Among his books are *Milton's Grand Style* (1963), the standard edition of Tennyson's poems (1969), a study of Tennyson (1972), and *Keats and Embarrassment* (1974).

SEAMUS HEANEY was born in 1939 in Co. Derry and was at Queen's University, Belfast, where he later became a lecturer in English. He has published five books of poems, and a *Selected Poems* appeared in 1980, along with *Preoccupations: Selected Prose*. He now lives in Dublin.

PETER PORTER was born in 1929 in Brisbane, Australia, and has lived in England since 1951. After several years of working in various jobs, including advertising, he became a freelance writer in 1968. His nine books of poetry include *Living in a Calm Country* (1975), *The Cost of Seriousness* (1978) and *English Subtitles* (1981). He has recently been Writer in Residence at Edinburgh University.

JOHN BETJEMAN was born in 1906, was at Magdalen College, Oxford, and has been Poet Laureate since 1972. He was knighted in 1969. He published his *Collected Poems* in 1958 (latest revised edition 1979), and more recently *Summoned by Bells, High and Low, A Nip in the Air* and *Church Poems*.

GAVIN EWART was born in 1916 and read classics at Christ's College, Cambridge. After army service during the war he worked for the British Council and then as an advertising copywriter. He has been a freelance writer since 1971. His first book of poems was published in 1939 and *The Collected Ewart 1933–1980* appeared in 1980.